SUGAR CREEK GANG
16
The HAUNTED HOUSE

Paul Hutchens

MOODY PUBLISHERS
CHICAGO

Original Title: *Haunted House at Sugar Creek*

ISBN-10: 0-8024-7020-3
ISBN-13: 978-0-8024-7020-1
Printed by Bethany Press in Bloomington, MN – 11/2010

We hope you enjoy this book from Moody Publishers.
Our goal is to provide high-quality, thought-provoking
books and products that connect truth to your real needs
and challenges. For more information on other books
and products written and produced from a biblical
perspective, go to www.moodypublishers.com or write to:

Moody Publishers
820 N. LaSalle Boulevard
Chicago, IL 60610

7 9 10 8 6

Printed in the United States of America

PREFACE

Hi—from a member of the Sugar Creek Gang!

It's just that I don't know which one I am. When I was good, I was Little Jim. When I did bad things—well, sometimes I was Bill Collins or even mischievous Poetry.

You see, I am the daughter of Paul Hutchens, and I spent many an hour listening to him read his manuscript as far as he had written it that particular day. I went along to the north woods of Minnesota, to Colorado, and to the various other places he would go to find something different for the Gang to do.

Now the years have passed—more than fifty, actually. My father is in heaven, but the Gang goes on. All thirty-six books are still in print and now are being updated for today's readers with input from my five children, who also span the decades from the '50s to the '70s.

The real Sugar Creek is in Indiana, and my father and his six brothers were the original Gang. But the idea of the books and their ministry were and are the Lord's. It is He who keeps the Gang going.

PAULINE HUTCHENS WILSON

1

I've been racking my brain, which is supposed to be under my red hair, trying to remember if I've ever told you the story of the haunted house at Sugar Creek and what happened there one night when we went on a coon hunt with Circus's dad's long-nosed, long-eared, long-legged, long-voiced, long-tongued hounds.

Circus is the name of the acrobatic member of our gang, and his dad is the father of a large family of nearly all girls and only one boy. His dad is the best hunter in all Sugar Creek territory.

The things that happened around and in and on top of that old haunted house would make any boy's red hair stand on end and also scare the living daylights out of him—which is what they did to me.

As I said, I've been racking my brain to see if I've ever told you about that haunted house, and I can't remember having written even half a paragraph about it. So here I go with that spooky, weird, and breathtaking story about the old abandoned house that was way up on a hill above Sugar Creek on some wooded property that belonged to Old Man Paddler.

Old Man Paddler is the kindest, friendliest, longest-whiskered old man who ever lived. He likes kids a lot and is always doing something that will make them happy or that will be good for them.

Of course, you know there isn't any such thing as a haunted house, which usually is supposed to be a house that nobody lives in but which is visited every now and then by a "ghost." Not a one of us believed in ghosts, except Dragonfly, the pop-eyed member of our gang. He is superstitious because his mother is.

When we heard about that old house in the woods and about the strange noises inside it that nobody could explain—well, it looked as if we were in for another exciting experience, different from any we'd had in our whole lives. It was while we were having a gang meeting one summer day on Bumblebee Hill that we first learned about it.

As quick as I had finished dinner that day, I looked across the table to where my grayish-brown-haired mom sat with my little sister Charlotte Ann in her lap.

My face must have had a question mark on it, because when Mom looked at me, she said the most surprising thing. I couldn't even imagine her saying it, it was so strange. She said, "Certainly, Bill, if you want to. I'm feeling just fine and not a bit tired. I can do the dishes alone for a change. So if you want to skip out and go down to your meeting with the gang, you just run along."

Imagine that! Mom nearly always expected me to do the dishes after every noon meal—

and so did Dad. And when both Mom and Dad expected me to do a thing, I nearly always did it, even when I didn't expect to myself.

I looked at Dad's big gray-green eyes under his shaggy brown eyebrows to see if Mom meant it, and if he was going to agree with her.

You could have knocked me over with a toothpick when he said, "That's right, Son, you run along to your gang meeting. Your mother and I have some things to talk over, and I'll knock off a little while from work and help her with the dishes myself."

Hearing him say that, and in such a way, made me suspicious that they wanted to get rid of me so they could talk about something that might especially interest me if I could hear it.

Still, I knew that in another minute I would dive for the screen door, shove it open, and make a wild dash across the yard. I would pass the big swing in our walnut tree, zip through the gate and across the graveled road, vault over the rail fence and run *swish-zip-zip-zippety-sizzle* down the path that had been made by barefoot boys' bare feet to the spring.

There I'd swerve to the right and dash up along another rail fence that bordered the top of a bluff just above the bayou. Then I'd swing right again and sprint to the foot of Bumble-bee Hill and up its lazy slope to the old abandoned cemetery at the top. There we were going to have our gang meeting just as soon after lunch that day as all the members of the gang could get away from their houses and get there.

But with both of my parents wanting me to get lost in a hurry so that they could talk about something, I suddenly wished I could hear what they were going to say. I knew it wasn't polite to "eavesdrop," so I decided I wouldn't. It was almost by accident that I heard part of what they said—just enough to make me curious and want to find out more.

Right away I excused myself, scooped up my straw hat from the floor, where it wasn't supposed to be, and swished out our east door, which in the summertime is always open to help get a breeze through the house.

I was going so fast that I was halfway across our grassy yard before I heard the screen door slam behind me. Then I also heard something else, and it was, "*Bill Collins!* Come back here and close the door like a gentleman!"

When Dad says it like that, I always obey in a hurry.

I was trying hard to learn to shut doors like a gentleman around our house, but not having any older brothers or sisters to set an example for me, it was kind of hard. The only examples I had were my dad and mom, and they always shut the screen doors carefully anyway.

Well, I put on the brakes quick, stopped before I got to the walnut tree, dashed back, opened the screen door again, and shut it like a gentleman, which means quietly.

Then I saw our pitcher pump standing at the end of the boardwalk that runs out toward our barn. I saw the drinking cup hanging on a wire hook on it. I decided to get a drink, because I always liked to hear the pump handle squeak when I pumped the pump.

After a cool gulp or two, I tossed what water was left in the cup out into a little puddle where maybe forty-seven yellow butterflies were getting a drink themselves. They were the kind of butterfly boys like to catch and also the kind that lay eggs on cabbage plants in the garden and whose worms hatch out of the eggs and eat up the cabbages. Those forty-seven—more or less—yellow butterflies all came to life quick and fluttered up in forty-seven different directions. Right away they started to light again all around the muddy edge of the little puddle of water.

I decided to go back past the screen door again, and just as I got there I stopped out of curiosity to find out if Mom and Dad were talking about me or something I had done and shouldn't have.

This is what I heard Dad's big gruff voice say: "Yes, it's too bad. Poor boy. He's got a tick and will have to have a doctor's care."

Who's got a tick—and what of it? I wondered, for there were all kinds of wood ticks around Sugar Creek and also different kinds up North, where we'd gone on a camping trip once.

Then I heard Mom say in her worried voice, which she sometimes uses when she is worrying out loud, "Yes, Theodore"—which is my dad's first name—"it's too terribly bad, and it's his parents' own fault. They're always pick-ing on him, and that's made him nervous."

"Poor Dragonfly," Dad's gruff voice said. "I wonder if I should have a talk with his father."

What they were saying didn't make sense at all. In my mind's eye I could see Dragonfly standing stark naked with both of his parents standing beside him, looking him over from head to toe and picking ticks off him, and Dragonfly not feeling well and having to go to the doctor. I wanted to call into the kitchen and ask Dad or Mom if Dragonfly was very sick, but instead I decided to run on down to the gang meeting, which I did.

Boy oh boy, I felt good as I dashed out across our grassy yard. I swerved out of the way when I came to the walnut tree, reached up and caught hold of the ropes on either side of the swing, swung myself up, leaped off, and dashed on through the gate past "Theodore Collins" on the mailbox. I made bare-feet tracks on the dust of the road as I vaulted over the rail fence, and away I went, feeling like a million dollars.

Even as I ran, I noticed the path was bor-dered on either side with wildflowers, such as buttercups, harebells, dandelions, oxeye daisies, and a lot of others. There were also mayapples, great big patches of them, with shining, light green leaves.

If there is anything in all the world that feels better than anything else, it is to run through a woods with bare feet on a shaded path, smelling sweet-smelling flowers and pine trees and seeing different-colored butterflies flitting around—and maybe scaring up a rabbit and watching it run *hoppety-sizzle* in some direction or other to get away from what it thinks is danger.

I stopped at the spring to get another cool drink and looked out across Sugar Creek. I noticed that it was very quiet, not having a ripple on it but only a lot of different-shaped splotches of foam, which I knew were clusters of very small air bubbles sticking together. For just a second I thought about how well I liked old Sugar Creek and how I would like to go in swimming right that very minute with the rest of the gang.

Then, as I hurried on up along the rail fence toward Bumblebee Hill, I decided that Sugar Creek's unruffled surface with those specks of foam scattered all over it was kind of like a boy's face with a lot of freckles on it, which was the kind of face I had.

Sugar Creek and I were pretty good friends, I thought, as I dashed on.

I must have gotten an earlier start than any of the rest of the gang, because, when I came to the bottom of Bumblebee Hill, there wasn't a one of them there. Instead of going on up to the cemetery at the top, I just lay down in the grass at the foot of the hill and waited, hating to go up to the cemetery all by myself for some reason, even though there wasn't any such thing in the world as a ghost.

For a while I lay on my back watching some big white clouds up there in the sky, which looked sort of like the snow-white packs of wool that Dad shears off our sheep and ties into big white bundles for selling. I thought about how interesting it would be if I could make a quick jump clear up there and float from one cloud to another as if I was as light as a feather. Then I got to thinking again about how white they were, like my mom's sheets hanging on the line on Monday, and from that I thought of my parents and Charlotte Ann and her almost-snow-white soft skin and how cute she was when Mom was washing her face.

That made me think of Dragonfly, and at that very second I felt an ant or something crawling on my hand. That reminded me of Dragonfly's ticks. Also, at the very same time, I heard somebody sneeze and heard feet running, and I knew Dragonfly himself was coming.

I rolled over quick and sat up and squinted at him, not being able to see him very well because of looking up into the bright blue sky and at the snow-white clouds.

"Hi, Dragonfly," I said and looked at him to see if he appeared to be in good health, and he did, and I was glad of it.

"Hi, yourself," he said and plopped himself down on the ground and panted a while. He wheezed a bit, because he had a little asthma in the summer.

I looked at him, and he looked at me with his dragonflylike eyes, and he reached out with his right hand and took hold of the fruit of a mayapple that grew close to where I'd been lying and started to pull it off. The lemon-shaped yellow fruit had been hanging the way the fruit of all mayapples do—from a little stem that was fastened at the fork of the mayapple stalk just under the spreading leaves.

"Did you ever taste one?" Dragonfly wanted to know and started to lift the round, smooth apple to his lips.

But all of a sudden he was interrupted by an excited small-boy voice calling out from somewhere not far away, "Hey, you, *stop!* May-apples are *poison!*"

Even without looking, I knew it was Little Jim, the littlest member of our gang. He came dashing up to where we were, and I noticed he had with him a wildflower guide, which was open to a picture of a pretty green mayapple illustration. Finding out all he could about wild-flowers and telling us about them whenever he found one he'd never found before—stuff like that—was one of Little Jim's hobbies.

Dragonfly didn't like to be stopped from doing what he wanted to do, so he bit into the mayapple. Then he screwed up his face into a homely twisted expression and spit out his bite quickly, drew his arm back, and hurled the rest of the apple up toward one of the white clouds that hung in the sky above Sugar Creek.

We all took a quick look at Little Jim's book, and I felt better when I read that "while the leaves and the stem of the mayapple are poisonous, the fruit is not, but tastes very sour."

There isn't anything much prettier in all Sugar Creek territory, though, than a bed of mayapples growing in a shady place under a tree, each stalk about a foot high, and each one having a snow-white flower with a yellow center. They were very nice to look at even though they weren't good to eat.

"Look," Little Jim said, "here's a flower that's blossomed late. It's supposed to blossom in May, you know. See, it's got six petals, and the center has exactly twice as many yellow stamens."

"So what?" Dragonfly asked, still with his lips puckered up and also rinsing out his mouth with saliva, which he spit out in the direction of Bumblebee Hill.

"They're *all* like that," Little Jim said. "Every one that's ever born has only *one* white flower on it, and every white flower has just six petals and exactly *twelve* yellow stamens in its center!"

"Who cares?" Dragonfly asked in a disgusted mumbling voice.

Little Jim knew that it was important. I understood that little guy like an open book, and I knew what he was thinking about. I didn't say anything with my voice but only with my eyes when he looked into my green ones with his very clear blue ones. In fact, I didn't say anything about what we were thinking until quite a while later—not till a lot later in this story, when we were having some excitement that made some of our adventures in other years look like two cents.

2

Pretty soon the rest of the gang was there: Circus, the acrobatic member; Big Jim, our leader and the oldest one of us and the fiercest fighter; Poetry, the roundest one of us, who was the most mischievous and also the one who knew 101 poems by heart and was always quoting one at the wrong time.

We all lay down in the tall grass in the old cemetery and for a while didn't do anything except just tumble around and act lazy—all except little Jim, who kept moseying around with his flower guide, looking for new wildflowers and marking a page in his book whenever he found one and also putting down the date, which was the tenth of July.

All of a sudden, Big Jim sat up, looked from one to the other of us, then startled us by asking, "You guys hear there's a haunted house up on a hill about a mile down the creek on the other side of Old Man Paddler's cabin?"

"There is not," the rest of us told him.

But Big Jim said, "Oh, there isn't, isn't there? Look." He pulled a piece of newspaper out of his pocket, which he unfolded quickly, and we saw a picture of a weird-shaped house that looked maybe a hundred years old. Weeds and vines were growing all around it, the steps were broken down, and torn blinds hung at dirty windows. Its front face had about the lonesomest expression I'd ever seen a house have—like a very sad old man who needed a haircut and a shave and was hungry and didn't have a friend in the world.

Big Jim read out loud from the newspaper, and as he read I got more and more interested, and so also did all of us. Dragonfly looked worried, and Little Jim's eyes got big and bright.

I studied the picture of the old house in Big Jim's hand and noticed that the paper was a copy of the *Sugar Creek Times*. I'd read the *Sugar Creek Times* every week for a long time, but I hadn't seen any picture in it such as that, and so I couldn't believe it.

"Let me see the date," I said. I reached for the paper, but Big Jim jerked his arm away and held the paper at arm's length.

Poetry, who happened to be lying in the direction in which Big Jim had stretched out his arm, grabbed the paper and held on, and in a minute we were all seeing the date.

It was a very old *Sugar Creek Times*, which had been printed forty years ago. It was yellow with age and musty smelling, but there it was as plain as day—a picture of an old stone house, and the news caption below it said—with a big question mark after it—

HAUNTED HOUSE?

I shifted my position, being uncomfortable

because of sitting on my left bare foot, and also because of sitting on something kind of hard, which didn't feel very good to sit on. I shoved my hand under me, worked my fingers down into the matted grass to see what it was, then rolled over quick. It was a flint arrowhead, the kind Indians used many years ago.

"Hey, gang, look what I found!" I said and held up the triangle-shaped, sharp-edged piece of rock for us all to see. Thinking about the haunted house and Dragonfly, I said in a serious voice, but with a mischievous grin in my mind, "This arrowhead was on the end of an arrow that maybe killed a lot of people a long time ago when Indians lived around here. One man probably was shot right here in the graveyard. And when he fell dead, he fell right where Dragonfly is lying now. The very minute he died, his ghost jumped up and started running around the country until it found a place to live, and when it saw that old house, it decided that was just the place, so it moved in!"

Poetry knew I was only trying to be funny, so he tried to be the same way and said in an excited voice, "Hey, Dragonfly, get up *quick!* You're lying on a ghost."

Well, it wasn't funny to Dragonfly. Poor little guy, he couldn't help it that he was superstitious, and maybe we shouldn't have kidded him about it. But we liked Dragonfly a lot, and Dad says if anybody kids you it's a sign he likes you and be sure not to get mad.

Dragonfly frowned instead of jumping as

we'd expected him to. He got a stubborn look on his face and said, "Yes, and as soon as the ghost found out that it was a ghost, it turned a somersault backwards and knocked the breath out of two or three people."

With that, Dragonfly came alive and made a backward somersault in our direction. The next thing I knew, Poetry and I were being bowled over and mauled as if a steamroller had hit us.

It was good fun, but we still weren't having quite as much fun as we wanted to, certainly not as much excitement, so we held a gang meeting to decide on something interesting to do.

"I move we go up into the hills to Old Man Paddler's cabin and let him tell us an exciting story," Little Jim said.

Circus said, "Second the motion," and in a jiffy we had all voted "Yes" and were on our way. It was always fun to go up to Old Man Paddler's clapboard-roofed cabin in the hills.

At the rate we ran, it took us only a little while to get to the spring, where we all stopped and got a drink.

Circus, the fastest runner of any of us, got there first and was down on his knees on a stone beside the bubbling spring when we arrived at the old linden tree and looked down at him.

"You guys," he called up to us. "Take a look at this!"

In a second I was down there beside Circus,

frowning at a track of some kind that looked a lot like a baby's small hand that had its fingers spread and had been pressed down flat in the mud.

Poetry came puffing down next, with the rest of the gang scrambling after him. The minute he saw the track, he said, "That's a *ghost's* tracks. Look, there are a whole lot of them. See there, Dragonfly?"

"It's a wild animal of some kind," Little Jim said.

For some reason, I felt a strange, creepy feeling going up and down my spine, the way I get when I'm beginning to be scared.

Then Big Jim let out a low, surprised whistle and said, "Look at *that*, will you? It's got one toe missing!"

"One *finger*, you mean," Poetry said, and either Big Jim or Poetry was right.

On the other side of the little cement pool that my dad had made there to hold the springwater—so that anytime anybody wanted to, he could dip in a pail or a cup and get a drink—was a stretch of mud. And the spread toes or fingers of some animal walking on the flat of its hands or feet had made maybe a dozen tracks there.

"Suppose it's maybe a bear?" Dragonfly wanted to know.

"Probably a monstrous coon," Circus said. "One that's been caught in a trap, maybe, and lost one of its toes."

I'd seen thousands of possum and squirrel

and rabbit and coon tracks in my life, but those were the strangest tracks I'd ever seen. And for some reason I was getting the most curious feeling in my mind that I'd had in a long time.

"Maybe it *is* a terribly big coon's tracks," Little Jim said.

I wished it was, but the tracks were too big for that, and they were too small for a bear, which we didn't have in Sugar Creek territory anyway. Also they looked too much as if they'd been made by a baby's hand, I thought, to be the tracks of any kind of vermin that lived in Sugar Creek.

Circus, who knew animal tracks better than any of the rest of us, acted worried. "It's too big for a coon," he decided, "but I know how to find out for sure."

"How?" we asked.

He said, "I'll go get old Blue Jay. If it's a coon, he'll open up with a wild bawl, and if it's something else, he'll just sniff at it and act lazy and disgusted and walk away."

"Who's old Blue Jay?" Dragonfly wanted to know.

Circus said, "It's dad's new bluetick coonhound, which he just bought. It won't take me more'n a jiffy. You guys stay right here, but don't you dare touch those tracks till old Jay's smelled them."

With that, Circus straightened up and scrambled *lickety-sizzle* up the little incline and past the linden tree. Seconds later I heard him running through the dead leaves and grass as fast as anything.

Suddenly Big Jim turned to me and said, "Want to go along, Bill?"

"Sure," Poetry said, "he wants to go. Go ahead and go with him, Bill."

Somehow I felt my redheaded temper starting to get warm, and I wanted to sock something or somebody. I knew they'd said that because all the gang had found out that one of Circus's many sisters, who was kind of ordinary-looking but was also kind of nice, had sent me a pretty card on my birthday. Also, she was the only one of the different-sized awkward girls that came to our school who sometimes smiled back at me across the schoolroom when I ought to be studying arithmetic and wasn't.

But I had already learned that if I acted bothered when the gang teased me like that, then they would tease me even worse, so I said, "Sure, I'll go. Want to go with me, Dragonfly?"

He looked up quickly from studying the tracks and shook his head "No" while his raspy voice said "Yes" at the same time. Then he shook his head "No" again, with a kind of ridiculous-looking twist of his neck, and started clambering up the incline toward the linden trees as fast as he could with me right after him.

At the top, we saw a flash of Circus's blue overalls in the path that scalloped its way up the creek to the Sugar Creek bridge. We yelled to him to wait, which he did, and pretty soon the three of us were running and panting and talking as we hurried along past oak and maple and beech and all other kinds of trees. Dragonfly was sneezing every now and then, because it was hay fever season and he always was allergic to a lot of things anyway, including ragweed and goldenrod, which grew all along the path.

I felt terribly bashful as we got close to Circus's house. All of a sudden I looked ahead and spied something like a girl out in their front yard. I noticed that she was about the size I was and was wearing a red dress that was almost exactly like the one my mom wears around the house sometimes and which Mom says is her favorite housedress. Mom had a pretty red print dress with a zipper front and a belt that tied in the back and two pockets up close to the neck, shaped like flowerpots.

When Circus ran ahead, all of a sudden I got an upside-down notion in my red head that I wanted to climb up on the rail fence that ran along the edge of Circus's lane and balance myself and walk on the top rail awhile. Before I could have stopped myself from doing it, even if I had known I was going to do it, I *was* doing it—walking along with my bare feet, balancing myself to keep from falling off. I managed to move in the direction of the red dress with the flowerpot pockets, although I was not able to see the dress very well because I had to watch where I was walking.

Everything would have been all right if I hadn't tried to see if I could stand on one leg and hold the other straight out in front of me and make a complete turn by hopping with the other foot. The next thing I knew, I was on the ground on the other side of the fence in Circus's pop's cornfield, feeling very foolish and wondering, *What on earth?*

I decided to stay there awhile and not let anyone see me, which I did, crawling on my hands and knees between the corn rows toward Circus's house. All of a sudden, I began to notice the tracks my hands were making in the soft brown dirt. They were almost exactly like those we'd seen at the spring at Sugar Creek, only of course they were a lot larger.

Then I heard Circus coming back. He had with him the prettiest hound I'd ever seen—a great big, large-boned, straight-legged dog with a silky black head and black ears and a blue-and-white tail that was shaped like a question mark or else maybe like the sickle my dad uses to cut weeds. The rest of the hound was darkish white with small blue spots all over him, clear down to the very end of his toes. The hound had the saddest, lazy expression I ever saw on a dog's face, but he had kind eyes that looked as though he thought a boy was a good friend.

I wished Little Jim were there. If there is anything he likes to do better than anything else it is to stroke a friendly dog on the head.

"Look!" Circus said after we'd been hurrying back up the creek toward the spring. He stopped, while we all caught our breath—especially Drag-onfly, who was slower because he had short breath. "See how long his ears are? His ear spread is twenty-four inches from the tip of one ear to the tip of the other."

Circus spread the dog's ears out like a boy spreading out the wings of a pigeon. The hound twisted its head sideways a little, reached up real quick, and licked Circus's hand. Then, because Circus's face happened to be close by, he got licked in the face with old Blue Jay's long red tongue.

"He's a genuine bluetick," Circus said. "Dad paid a hundred dollars for him. He's the best coonhound we ever had, and he won't chase anything *except* coons."

"What makes you call him a bluetick?" Dragonfly asked, and I noticed, as he said it, that he twisted his neck again, funnylike.

Circus said, "Because of these little blue spots all over him. That's the name dog experts give to that kind of a dog."

Well, pretty soon we were there, and Circus took old Blue Jay, with his sickle tail over his back, down the incline to the spring at the base of the leaning linden tree. The rest of us watched to see what he'd do when he smelled the strange-looking tracks.

"It's pretty nearly bound to be a coon," Circus said, "because coons always wash their food before they eat it, and this great big terrible old coon probably stopped there and washed his breakfast this morning."

I knew coons did that, so I thought maybe Circus was right.

I don't know what I expected Blue Jay to do when he got to the base of the old linden tree and started to smell the funny-looking hand-like tracks of the animal or ghost or whatever it was. I remembered that, even before we got there, Circus had said Blue Jay was a very special kind of coon dog and that you could tell by the sound of his bawl when he was on a trail just what kind of vermin he was following. You could also tell by the sound of his bark whether he was still trailing or whether he had chased the coon or whatever it was to a tree or a den. On the trail it was one kind of bark, and when he was "treed" it was another.

But I certainly didn't expect to hear such a *weird* dog voice.

The very minute Blue Jay's nose came within a foot or two of those strange tracks, he began acting very excited and half mad—like a boy when he has walked with his bare feet through a patch of nettles, and his feet and legs itch so much that he can't stand it.

Old Blue Jay sniffled and snuffled with a noise like a very small boy who has a cold but doesn't have any handkerchief. The blue-ticked hair on his back stood up, the way a dog's hair does when he is angry at another dog or a person or a cat. He didn't act at all as I'd seen dogs act when they strike an animal's trail and are trying to decide which way it has gone so as to start following it.

He lifted his long nose off the ground and let out a long, high-pitched wail that sounded almost like a ghost is supposed to sound at midnight in a haunted house beside an abandoned graveyard.

The next thing I knew, he had leaped across the puddle of water on the other side of the spring and was running along the edge of Sugar Creek, following the path that ran in the opposite direction from the swimming hole, straight toward the old sycamore tree and the cave. Every few seconds he let out a long, very weird-sounding high-pitched cry. I knew that if I heard it at night along Sugar Creek, it would send cold, bloodcurdling chills up and down my spine—which it was doing right that very minute anyway.

I had followed a coon chase on quite a few different nights when the Sugar Creek Gang had gone hunting with Circus's pop and his long-nosed, long-voiced, long-eared, long-tongued, long-legged, long-tailed dogs, and I was all set to follow old Blue Jay on a daytime hunt.

That hound certainly was a fast trailer. Quick as anything, he was nose-diving up and down the hill, wherever the trail went. Pretty soon he was bawling and running as fast as anything straight down the path toward the old hollow sycamore tree, which grows at the edge of the swamp and where our gang had so many exciting experiences.

We galloped along after him, stopping now and then when it seemed he had lost the trail. Whenever he lost it, he began running around in every direction, circling chokecherry shrubs and papaw bushes and wild rosebushes and brier patches and diving in and out of little thickets until he found the trail again. But he still kept going in the general direction of the swamp and the sycamore tree.

"It's a coon," Big Jim said, "and it's heading for the old sycamore tree."

"How can you tell it's a coon?" Dragonfly said from behind us, running as close to me as he could and having a hard time to keep up.

"Yeah, how can you?" Poetry puffed from beside me somewhere.

And Big Jim said, "I can't for sure, but he acts as crazy as a coon dog is supposed to act when it's on a coon trail."

Well, I knew that Circus, who knew more about his dad's hound than any of the rest of us did, would maybe know, so I asked him.

He said between puffs as he dashed along with me, "I don't know. If it's a coon, I'd think it wouldn't go in such crazy circles."

3

Soon we came to the old North Road, and there Blue Jay ran into trouble. He leaped over the rail fence as if he weighed only twenty pounds instead of ninety-five and began running up and down the side ditches on both sides of the road, acting worried and trying to find where "whatever it was" had gone.

Little Jim spoke up and said, "I'll bet if it made those tracks at the spring *early* this morning when it was washing its breakfast, and that if it crossed the road here a whole lot later, a lot of different cars and horses and wagons have run over the tracks, and Jay can't smell 'em."

"Yeah," Circus said, "but they didn't run out in the ditch on the other side of the road."

Try as he would, old Blue Jay couldn't find the trail. It was as if the coon or "whatever it was" had come to the road here and then just disappeared.

After five or ten minutes of worried circling and whimpering, Blue Jay came back to where we were, looked up at Circus, and whined as much as to say, "Well, that's that. What do we do next? I give up."

Dragonfly spoke up then, and I noticed that his voice had a sort of tremble in it as he said, "M—maybe when it got here, it stopped walking, and began floating in the air like ghosts do."

I looked at his dragonflylike eyes, and that little spindle-legged guy had an expression on his face that said he actually wondered if maybe it *had* been a ghost!

Although we kept on trying to get Blue Jay interested, we couldn't. He just acted as though it was all over, so all of us went on down past the sycamore tree and up into the hills to Old Man Paddler's house, as we'd planned to do in the first place, to get him to tell us an exciting story. We took Blue Jay along so we wouldn't have to go all the way back to Circus's house with him and also so we could get to Old Man Paddler's house quicker.

We didn't stay very long at Old Man Paddler's cabin because it seemed we had interrupted him in his work. He must have heard us coming, just as we were stopping to get a drink at the spring that comes tumbling out of the rocky hillside below his house. He opened the wooden door and just stood there quietly, without moving or saying a word at first.

I had finished getting a drink and was looking around to see if there were any ghost's tracks or any other kind, and there weren't. Then I'd heard the door open.

I looked at the old-fashioned clapboard-roofed cabin with the white-whiskered old man standing in the open doorway. In a flash my mind was seeing a picture in our Bible story-book at home of a man named Moses. He was a very important person to whom God had given the Ten Commandments, which every boy in the world ought to learn by heart and also ought to obey.

In just that minute he was standing there, I remembered some of the different places I'd seen him and what he'd been doing. Once we'd saved his life, you know, which I told you about in the very first story of the Sugar Creek Gang. Also, every Sunday morning in the church we all went to, that old man would come in and sit down close to the front, sometimes coming just a little late.

Sometimes some of us boys weren't as quiet in church as we should have been. We were always so glad to see each other and to be together and to tell each other different things that we had a hard time keeping still even in church. We are learning to, though, because a church building is a house of worship. But even though I knew Jesus was my Savior, and I was learning to like Him better than anything in the world, I still had a hard time sitting still.

But when that kind old man with his long whiskers and his very neatly combed silky white hair would come in and take his seat, it sort of seemed that God Himself had come into the church and it was time to start being quiet and reverent.

Well, when Old Man Paddler saw us there at his spring he called out, "Hello, boys! Come on in and have some sassafras tea!"—which is exactly what we hoped he would say.

In a few minutes we were in his cabin, sitting around on different chairs and on the bottom step of the old wooden stairway that leads up to his loft. We were sitting or half lying down on the floor while he stirred up the fire in his cookstove and heated the water a little hotter.

While the old man dropped little red chips of sassafras roots in the kettle of hot water, and we were chattering and half wrestling with each other as boys do, I looked around a little. The very first thing I noticed was his map on the wall above the kitchen table. It was a map of the world and had different-colored pins stuck in different places on it. That old man had friends all over the world, most of them missionaries. Nearly everybody at Sugar Creek knew he kept that map on his wall so that he could be reminded to pray for the different people.

"I was just about ready to stop work, boys," his kind, trembling voice said as he moved around, setting out seven blue-flowered cups and saucers on the table. I noticed there was a brand-new oilcloth on it with a checkerboard design, which would make a great checkerboard for Dad and me to play checkers on during a winter night at our house. Dad and I play that game a lot. Another thing I noticed over on a corner of the table was a tablet of yellow paper like the kind we often used at school.

It was what the tablet said on the front cover that made Dragonfly ask the question he did. And that started Old Man Paddler telling us about ghosts and also about Old Tom the Trapper of the Sugar Creek of long ago, whom an Indian had shot with an arrow.

Dragonfly, who is always seeing things first anyway, saw the writing on the tablet and nudged me. I looked, and this is what I saw:

"THE CHRISTIAN AFTER DEATH,"
by Seneth Paddler

And I knew he was maybe writing a book for somebody to publish.

Just as he always does when he wants to know something, Dragonfly spoke up without waiting to think first. "Mr. Paddler, do you believe in ghosts?"

You could have knocked me over with a drop of sassafras tea when he asked that question, but a little later I was glad he had, because it was that question that got the old man started on the story of Old Tom the Trapper.

"I'll tell you a ghost story in just a minute," he said. He looked around at us with his twinkling gray-green eyes. I could tell that, if his whiskers hadn't been in the way, I could have seen a smile on his face. When a man has a twinkle in his eyes like that, he is thinking something pleasant. Even if he doesn't have a smile on his *face* he maybe does have one in his mind.

"It tastes just like a bright red melted lollipop," Little Jim said, while he swished his cup around and sipped his last sweet drop of sassafras tea, while most of the rest of us did the same thing.

"You see," the old man said, when he started his story, "Old Tom was a very kind old man who lived about a mile from here on a little hill above Sugar Creek. He made his living by trapping muskrat and raccoon and beaver and other fur-bearing animals. My twin brother, Kenneth, and I were boys at the time, and we used to go over to Old Tom's house once in a while to see him and to hear him tell stories, just like you boys come to see me.

"There were quite a few Indians living about a mile farther on, and they were hunting and trapping, too. They and Old Tom were pretty good friends—that is, *most* of the Indians liked him. But one big half-breed Indian, named War Face, decided Tom was catching too much fur. He used to sneak down along the creek right after Tom had set his traps and 'throw' them, so he wouldn't catch anything. Sometimes game would be stolen right out of Tom's traps, and that worried the old man a lot.

"Old Tom was one of the best Christians that ever lived, I guess, and he was always reading his Bible and *Pilgrim's Progress* and some books by George Eliot, and it made him feel pretty bad that somebody was stealing from his traps. Well, he didn't know who was doing it until one day he wrote a little note and tied it to a branch not far from the place where he had one of his traps set. And that note said, 'Remember, whenever you are about to do something wrong, that Somebody is watching you.'

"Old Tom spelled that word 'Somebody' with a capital S, and you boys know that Old Tom meant that *God* was watching. Tom thought maybe that would make the thief stop and think, and then maybe he wouldn't do any more poaching.

"Well, next morning Old Tom found a note tied to the knob of his cabin door, which said, 'Any traps set on the west side of the North Road will be thrown, and any fur caught will be taken. Somebody will be watching you.'

"Old Tom didn't know what to do. The best trapping was on the west side nearer the swamp, and he'd been trapping there for years. But he was very kind and didn't like to quarrel with anybody, so he decided to go see War Face to talk things over.

"He started out very early that same morning, following his trapline. He had maybe a dozen traps on the west side. He'd made his mind up that if he had caught anything during the night he wouldn't take it until he'd talked with War Face. But when he passed one of his traps, about a hundred yards west of the road, it had a red fox in it. Because Old Tom had a very tender heart and couldn't stand to see anything suffer unnecessarily, he decided to stop and kill the fox before going on.

"And that's where it happened, boys," Old Man Paddler said. He lifted his blue-flowered cup and looked at it as though his thoughts were far away. Then he looked out his kitchen window down toward the spring.

I was sitting on the edge of my chair, waiting to hear the rest of the story, feeling sorry for Old Tom and hoping maybe the story would end without his getting killed, but it didn't.

A second later Old Man Paddler went on, and this is what he said: "Tom had just killed the fox and straightened up to look around and go on when an arrow came whizzing out from behind the bushes up the shore. It struck him in the breast, and the arrowhead went clear through and came out his back.

"And there Kenneth and I found him when we happened along a little later. He died in just a little while but not until he'd had a chance to tell us the story.

"'Bury me under the big tree beside my new house,' he managed to gasp out, just before he stopped breathing."

There was a little more to the story, which I won't take time to tell you now, but I was thinking about that arrow and wondering what had become of it, so I watched for a chance to ask a question, which was, "What became of the arrow?"

He didn't seem to be much interested in that, but he said, "Kenneth and I kept it, but one day it got mislaid and was accidentally burned in the fireplace. We saved the arrowhead and kept it for years until one day we lost it."

Dragonfly seemed interested in Old Tom. He asked, "Where did they bury him?"

"Just where he wanted them to—under the maple tree beside his new stone house."

I guess we all gasped at once when he said that, and Big Jim spoke up real quick and said, "*Stone* house? Where?"

"About a mile down the creek. I went to see it one day last week. There's a regular jungle around the house now with the whole place overgrown with weeds and bushes and shrubs."

Up to that minute Old Man Paddler hadn't told us anything about any ghost, so Dragonfly said, "What about the *ghost* you were going to tell us about?"

Old Man Paddler focused his gray-green eyes on Dragonfly's dragonflylike eyes and said, "That's where a lot of people think a ghost lives—in that old house. You see, boys, about twenty years ago a man and his wife moved into it and lived there a while until the woman found out about Old Tom having been buried under the maple tree. After that, whenever she heard noises in the woods at night, she imagined it was Old Tom's ghost walking around. So they moved out, and the house has been empty ever since. No one seems to want to live in the woods so far away from where other people live, I suppose. A few years ago a tornado twisted the barn off its foundation and blew down a lot of trees, so it's more forsaken-looking than ever. But the old maple tree under which Tom was buried still stands."

Old Man Paddler stopped talking, looked at us, and said, "Tom's in heaven now, boys, where all saved people go, you know."

Dragonfly wasn't satisfied. "Did the woman *really* hear sounds in the woods?"

"Of course not," Big Jim said.

But the old man startled us by saying, "There are a lot of folks around Sugar Creek who believe she did. It's hard to get people *not* to believe a house is haunted once the story gets going."

Listening to the old man talk and thinking about ghosts gave me a creepy feeling. I didn't believe in ghosts myself, no sir, but before we left the cabin, I knew that one of the very first things the gang was going to do was hike up to that old stone house and see the big tree under which Old Tom the Trapper was buried. I just knew that if we went up there, we'd find something very interesting. Also, we might run into a very exciting adventure of some kind.

It was too late to go that afternoon, though, because the house was so far down the creek and in a territory where none of us had gone before.

On the way back to the spring, we decided to stop at the old swimming hole and have a swim before we went to our different homes. We went by the North Road bridge, and Big Jim picked out the place that we thought might be the exact spot where Old Tom had been shot with the arrow.

As boys sometimes do when they read or

hear an interesting story, we decided to act out the story of "Old Tom the Trapper." We let Little Jim and Dragonfly be the twin brothers Kenneth and Seneth Paddler, and Circus was the half-breed Indian War Face. Poetry was the red fox that got caught in a trap, and I was going to be Old Tom the Trapper and get shot through the chest with an arrow.

Big Jim took the part of the director of the play and told each one of us what to do and when to do it.

Circus hid himself back in the bushes, and Poetry stuck his hand in a forked branch as though it was caught in a trap.

Then I came whistling through the woods along the creek till I came to Poetry, who was lying on his stomach and whimpering like a caught fox. When I got to where he was, I made myself act sad, and I said, "Oh, you poor, poor little foxie! I feel so sorry for you, but you've been eating up all my chickens, and besides I need your fur to help make a living."

Poetry looked up, made a face at me, and said with a mischievous grin in his voice, "If you kill me, I'll turn into a fox's ghost and yelp and bark at you all the rest of your life."

"I won't *have* any life," I said. "I'll be dead in just another minute."

I picked up a stick, and pretended to sock Poetry with it, and he, being a good actor, stiffened out and acted as if he was dying. Then, just as I straightened up—*whizz!*—Circus threw a mayapple at me from behind the bushes. Even though I tried to dodge, it hit me *ker- squash* on the chest and spattered itself and its insides all over my shirt.

"Help!" I yelled, mad at Circus for actually throwing something at me. I plopped myself down to the ground beside my dead fox and groaned and held one hand to my chest—holding in my other hand the flint arrowhead that I'd found back in the cemetery.

Lying there, waiting for Kenneth and Seneth Paddler to come and find me just before I died, I got to thinking, what if I was *actually* dead? I knew enough of the Bible from what Dad and Mom had read out loud at our house, and from what I'd heard our minister preach, and from what I'd memorized in a contest we'd had in school, and from what I'd learned in Sunday school, and from reading my own New Testament—I knew that if I was an honest-to-goodness Christian myself, when I died I'd go right straight to heaven to be where Jesus is.

I lay on my back groaning and moaning, looking up at the very pretty sky, which had long, wrinkled white clouds running almost all the way across it. It was what our schoolbooks called a mackerel sky but which reminded me of my mom's washboard. And I thought of the Bible verse that says, ". . . absent from the body . . . at home with the Lord."

I shut my eyes and imagined myself to be Old Tom the Trapper's spirit up there, looking down at my body lying beside a dead red fox and seeing the long arrow clear through my chest. Then my imagination turned a somersault, and I was looking down at a very chubby boy with his hand in the fork of a branch, and beside him was a red-haired boy who had two large upper front teeth, a million freckles on his face, and smashed mayapple stains on his shirt, and I thought how ridiculous we looked.

But then I let my thoughts take me real quick up into heaven where Jesus is, and for just a second I imagined I saw Him running to meet me and calling me by name and saying, "Welcome, Bill Collins! I appreciate very much your being a friend of Mine while you were down on the earth. I died for you down there upon the cross, and I'm glad you decided, while you were still a boy, to give your heart to Me."

That was as far as I got to think, because right then I heard steps running along Sugar Creek. I looked quick, and it was blue-eyed Little Jim and spindle-legged Dragonfly hurrying toward me.

Well, that was as much of the story of Old Tom the Trapper as we got to act out that day. The rest of it, where Old Tom got buried under a big maple tree beside the haunted house, we'd have to act out some other day when we had lots of time—which we decided ought to be the next week.

4

The first thing Mom said to me when I got home that late afternoon was "Bill, come in the house a minute. I need a little help!" Her voice sounded as if I wasn't as good a boy as I hoped I was.

I had just come through the front gate and had shut it, and Poetry and I were standing up in our big rope swing under the walnut tree, swinging and pumping ourselves higher and higher. At the same time we were talking to each other in panting breaths and dreaming out loud to each other about the haunted house and Old Tom the Trapper's buried body under the maple tree. Poetry and I certainly liked each other a lot and always hated to have to leave each other and come out of our boys' world and be part of our families again.

So when Mom's impatient voice called to me from the side porch, it was like having a nice ice cream cone knocked out of my hand just after I'd taken a few bites.

There was something in my mother's tone of voice that seemed to say that maybe I should have come home sooner and that she had had too many things to do all day while I hadn't done much of anything except play.

For a second, I was half mad, so I yelled

back from away up in the air where I was at the time and said to her, "Can't a boy have a little time to himself?"

And then all of a sudden, while Poetry and I swooped down with the cool wind blowing in my face and my shirt sleeves and overalls' legs flapping in the breeze the way they do when I'm swinging in a high swing, I saw Poetry's forehead get a frown on it. It was as though he was disgusted with my mom for calling me in a scolding voice, and I thought he was going to say something to her himself.

I certainly got a surprise when he said what he did say, which was, "She's an awfully nice mother. Let's both go in and help her."

Back and forth, back and forth, up and down, up and down, *whizz, whizz, whee . . .*

I was mad at Poetry for saying that, even though I knew it was the truth. And for a minute what we were doing wasn't a bit of fun. Mom *was* an awfully nice mother—in fact, maybe the best mother in all Sugar Creek or the whole world, I thought. But—well. I just didn't feel very good, so I quit pumping Poetry. He quit pumping me, too, and in a few sad jiffies our swing had stopped enough for us to get off.

I was still mad and mixed up in my mind, so I picked up a rock and threw it at our old red rooster. He was standing on top of a chicken coop in the barnyard, crowing as if he was very happy and also as though he didn't have a thing in the world to do, such as work, and that he was glad of it.

My rock hit the roof of the coop, glanced off, and went on toward the barn. It bounced along a half-dozen times before it finally hit the side of the barn just below the open window where our cat, Mixy, was sitting sunning herself.

The old red rooster jerked, and his crowing noise ended with a scared squawk. Mixy jumped as though she had been shot and made a dive for inside the barn. And at the same time I heard my dad's voice thunder at me from the grape arbor on the other side of our iron pitcher pump and say, *"How many times have I told you not to throw rocks at Andrew Jackson?"*—that being our old red rooster's name.

"I'll see you tomorrow," Poetry said all of a sudden. He turned and picked up a corncob that was lying there and threw it toward our front gate and then ran to pick it up again and go on through the gate and start down the road toward his house.

Well, it was a sad way to end a very wonderful afternoon, and it seemed my parents were to blame for it. I let myself be pretty mad for a minute. And when a red-haired boy gets mad, it's hard to get over it for a while. I knew a Bible verse, which I'd learned once in a Bible memory contest in our school, that said, "Do not let the sun go down on your anger," which means to be sure to get your temper over with before night.

I took a quick look at the sun, which was just above Dad's head as he stood there by the grape arbor, and I knew I had maybe an hour yet before the sun would go down. The way I felt that very second, it seemed it would take a lot longer than that.

"What time is it?" I yelled to Mom, still thinking about how long it would be before the sun would go down.

And she said from the side porch, "It's time to gather the eggs," and Dad said from under the grape arbor, "It's time to start the chores."

I picked up another rock, wanting to throw it at something, which is what a boy likes to do when he's half mad. But I just stood there looking at my dad and also down at my bare feet, which were digging themselves into the sand of the driveway.

And just then I looked down the road toward Poetry. He was walking backward, watching in our direction to see what was going to happen, if anything.

He saw me looking, and I whirled real quick, with my rock still in my hand, made a wide sweep with my arm to throw it across the road into the woods, and—well, it happened again! That crazy rock went low and sailed right straight toward our tin mailbox, which has my dad's name, "Theodore Collins," on it. *Wham!* It struck that box right in the center, making a terribly loud noise.

Then it bounced back toward me, having made a big dent in the box, and there I was—in Dutch with my parents and mad at both of them and at myself.

What can a boy do at a time like that? I certainly didn't know what, but I had to do something. So I just stood there, looking at the dent in the mailbox and saying and doing nothing until Dad said, "You can come on in the house a minute, William"—William being the name he uses on me instead of Bill whenever I've done something I shouldn't.

I looked around quick for something to pick up and carry with me, such as a stick or a twig—not to protect myself but to have something to hold onto. I felt maybe like a drowning person feels when he looks around in the water for something to hold onto and, seeing a little stick or even a floating straw, makes a grab for it.

My eyes spied a branch about two feet long, and I quick picked it up and carried it with me, swishing it around and striking at a swarm of gnats that were in front of my face.

The sun was getting lower, I thought, and there were three tempers that would have to hurry up and get over with before it went down—Mom's and Dad's and mine.

All of a sudden, I thought I saw a way to help Dad's temper and maybe Mom's too, so I said quicklike and as cheerfully as I could, "I'll get the eggs as fast as I can!" Whirling around, I made a dive out across the barnyard for the barn, dodging the chicken coop where old Andrew Jackson had been crowing a little while before.

But I was like one of Circus's hounds on a

leash, which tries to run but gets stopped quickly when it gets to the end of the leash. My dad's voice was like a leash when he said. "Stop! Come here!"

For some reason I did, all of a sudden realizing that the branch in my hand would make a fine switch for Dad to use on me and dropping it as if it had been a very hot potato.

Well, it's the most terrible feeling in the world to be on the "outs" with your parents. I'd been that way a few times in my life, and I didn't know what to do. I actually hadn't done anything wrong on purpose, but all of a sudden I realized I *had* been thinking only about myself and what fun I could have and not about how tired Mom might be and how she might need help. Even though I hated to admit it, I knew I was wrong.

"Bring the switch with you," Dad said.

I stooped, picked it up, and carried it to him, walking sideways and striking at different things and not looking at his gray eyes below his shaggy reddish-brown eyebrows or at his reddish-brown mustache.

I knew I was in for something. I had been told plenty of times not to throw rocks at our chickens or any of our cows or pigs or sheep or horses and also not at Theodore Collins's name on our mailbox.

Suddenly Dad said in a very pleasant voice, "You're getting to be a good shot, Bill. You going to be a pitcher on the Sugar Creek School ball team this fall when school starts?"

What on earth? I thought. *Why such a kind voice?*

"I didn't do it on purpose," I said. "I just wanted to throw a rock. I—"

"I know it," Dad said. "I used to feel like that myself when I was a boy."

For some reason, though, I still didn't feel good. It seemed Dad thought *Mom* was to blame for calling me in such a scolding voice, and I didn't like Mom to have to feel sad. I looked quick at her, and—would you believe it? —she had a smile on her face. She looked at Dad a minute; their eyes just looked and looked at each other. It was as though they were thinking kind of friendly things to each other and also liked each other a lot. My grayish-brown-haired mom and my reddish-brown-haired dad were wonderful parents, I thought, and I was awfully glad they liked each other.

In minutes the storm I had thought was coming was all over, and we were a happy family again. Neither one of my parents even mentioned the chicken coop or the mailbox. All of us were working like a house afire to get the chores done.

I helped Mom awhile first because my sister, Charlotte Ann, was too terribly little to do housework. First, I did one of the most important chores Mom ever lets me do around the house, which was to water her African violets— pretty green-leafed plants with bluish-purple flowers, which she grows in some very rich soil in a dish and keeps on the window ledge in our north window. An African violet is the kind of flower that has to grow in the shade without any direct sunshine on it. When you water it, you don't dare put even a drop on its leaves unless the water and the air in the room are about the same temperature. You have to very carefully pour the water on the soil itself or down where the roots are.

Even while I was squirting in a little water at a time with the eye dropper that I always used, I heard Mom humming a song of some kind in the kitchen. It was one we sometimes used in church, and the chorus goes: "Wonderful, wonderful Jesus, in the heart He implanteth a song . . ."

For some reason, as I looked down at the pretty bluish-purple flowers with their gold centers, I felt very happy. It seemed my parents were treating *me* like an African violet. Instead of putting cold water on me by scolding me and punishing me a lot, they were sort of watering my heart. I don't know how to explain it, but I could feel that they were pretty smart parents, and I liked them a terrible lot.

Next day, when Little Jim and I were talking, he said to me, "Mom lets me water her Saintpaulia, too."

"Let's you do what to her *what*?" I said.

And he said, "That's the Latin name of the African violet. I saw it in a book—*Saintpaulia*."

Well, pretty soon most of the chores were done, and we were having supper while it was still daylight, and the sun was still not down. It was what Dad said at the table when he asked the blessing that got me started to thinking again about the stone house and Old Tom the Trapper and ghosts.

This is what Dad said in his big, deep-toned voice, "Please bless Old Man Paddler as he writes his book on 'The Christian After Death.'"

For a minute my thoughts left Dad and the kitchen table filled with our good supper. I was again thinking about a dead red fox and an arrow sticking through Old Tom's chest. I thought of the stone house and of how wild Circus's dad's new bluetick hound had acted when he first smelled the strange-looking tracks at the spring.

Dad had finished his prayer, and he and Mom were talking about Old Man Paddler, before I interrupted them with an important question. Mom had just said, "You know, I think that old man is a genius. It's almost uncanny the things he knows about the Bible and everything else. I'll bet it'll be a wonderful book."

"You know what James Russell Lowell said a genius is, don't you?" Dad said to her.

Mom said, "No, what?"

Dad said, "Talent is that which is in a man's power; genius is that in whose power a man is" —something like that. I couldn't understand it, but I knew it was important.

Anyway, I piped up and said, "Our gang is going to visit Old Tom the Trapper's grave next week—can we?"

Dad came out of his grown-up world quick

and said, "You're going to visit Old Tom the Who's what?"

"Old Tom the Trapper's grave under the big maple tree beside the old haunted house."

Dad quickly looked at Mom, and Mom at Dad, and both of them at me. I looked down at my plate and scooped my fork under a pile of raw-fried potatoes and started to take a bite. Some of the thin slices fell off the fork on the way up to my mouth.

"Too big a bite, Bill," Mom said, and I frowned, knowing it before she told me.

Just that second, Charlotte Ann made a whimpering noise in the other room—she'd been napping. Mom excused herself, got up from the table to go in and see what was wrong, and Dad and I were alone for a minute.

"Who told you about Old Tom?" Dad asked.

"Old Man Paddler," I answered. "We were up to see him today."

Dad sipped his coffee, then said, "Well, if he told you, it must be all right for you to know. You going to take Dragonfly along?"

"Sure," I said, "that's one reason why we're going—to prove to him there isn't any such thing as a ghost. He's afraid of ghosts."

"You know what Sophocles said about fear, don't you?" Dad said.

I looked at Dad's eyes and grinned. He was always quoting what some famous somebody said about something. He was always reading and remembering things, and he and Mom often talked about them to each other.

I answered him by saying, "Who said what about what?"

He grinned. "What Sophocles said about fear. Didn't you say Dragonfly was afraid of ghosts?"

"Who's Sopho—what's his name?"

"Sophocles? He was a Greek poet."

"What's he got to do with Dragonfly?" I asked, feeling rather important because Dad was talking to me as if I were a grown-up.

"Nothing except that Sophocles said, 'To him who is in fear, everything rustles.'"

"I still don't see what that's got to do with Dragonfly and ghosts," I said, just as Mom came in with my little sister on her arm.

Charlotte Ann was yawning and acting as if she had just waked up. She was as cute as anything. Her small ears looked like a couple of little dried peaches glued onto the sides of her head.

Dad answered me by saying, "Nothing in particular, except that when you get to the haunted house, everything Dragonfly hears will sound like a ghost—the wind in the leaves, the rubbing of a tree branch against another, the snapping of a twig, everything."

Well, supper was soon over, and I felt wonderful inside. Both my parents liked me and didn't hold it against me that I had talked sassy to Mom, and Dad acted as though it was all right for the gang to go see the haunted house.

Just as I was passing Mom's chair to go outdoors awhile, I stopped and looked down at

Charlotte Ann's pretty soft pink cheeks and said to her, "You're a nice little girl. I hope when you grow up you won't talk back to your mother like your big, ugly, freckled-faced brother did today."

Mom, without looking at me at all, reached out and caught me by my overalls' suspender and pulled me a little closer. For a minute I stood there beside her with her arm around me. Well, it was the most wonderful feeling in the world to feel the way I felt right then.

Almost right away I was out the kitchen door, dashing toward the barn, picking up sticks and rocks and things and throwing them in different directions but not hitting anything, because I was especially careful not to throw them at anything.

Next week, I thought, when the gang had its next meeting, we'd all go up past Old Man Paddler's cabin and on down the creek into a territory we'd never visited before. I'd make certain Dragonfly was with us, so we could prove to him that there wasn't any such thing as a ghost. There we'd finish playing the game of Old Tom the Trapper.

That night, just before I crawled into my upstairs bed, I looked out under the rustling leaves of the ivy that hangs across the upper half of my window. Looking out into the garden with the moon shining on it, I thought about what a pretty moonlight night it was. It felt good to think that God had made such a pretty world, and it seemed for a minute that I liked Him even better than I did my parents. I quickly dropped on my knees the way my parents had taught me to do when I was little and said a short prayer.

Then I crawled into bed and went to sleep.

I had a crazy kind of dream, though, and part of it was about Circus's new bluetick hound. Dragonfly was picking at all those little blue spots on him, and in my dream each spot was a small blue wood tick that Dragonfly was picking off.

And the next thing I knew it was morning.

5

Our gang had acted out a lot of stories, each one of us taking the part of one of the characters and having what our parents called "innocent fun." In fact, it seemed that I was pretending to be someone or something else nearly all the time. Sometimes I was a bear that growled and crawled around on the floor of our house. Once, when I was smaller, I was a fire engine and raced from one room of our house to another and up and down the stairs, making a fire-engine noise that must have sounded awful to Mom, because she stopped me and let me go outdoors.

Well, next week finally came, and the gang started out to finish playing Old Tom the Trapper. First, we stopped at the North Road bridge, and I got shot through the chest again. Then, because it would be too far for the gang to carry my dead body all the way to Old Tom's stone house, I came to life until we got there.

Old Man Paddler had drawn a map for us so that we wouldn't get lost, and after about an hour of walking we finally arrived. It certainly was a spooky-looking place. It was way up on a bluff above Sugar Creek and had a lot of maple and ash and elm and other kinds of trees all around it and ivy clinging to one of the walls.

The heavy wooden door looked strong enough to keep out Indians or wild animals. The barn, about a hundred feet away from the house, was twisted into a very ugly shape and was half lying down. There was an old windmill near the house that didn't have any wheel at the top. The wheel was lying twisted up and partly buried in the dirt at the bottom of the tower.

We walked all around, listening and imagining different things, and then the gang decided to bury me out under the great big maple tree, which was almost two feet thick at the base and had wide-spreading branches covered with large green heart-shaped leaves about the size of Dad's hand when it's spread out.

"All right," Big Jim, who was the director of our play, said. "Lay the poor old man right there till we have his grave ready."

I plopped my body down on the ground right where I was, made myself limp, and made the gang carry me to where they wanted me. They half dragged me to the base of the tree and left me lying alone, while they took some sticks and pretended to dig a grave. I was lying on maybe a hundred and fifty two-winged maple seeds that looked like the brass key we use to wind the eight-day clock in the kitchen. I was also lying on a root that felt awfully hard in the small of my back. So I rolled over once and then lay very quiet.

I watched what was going on out of the corner of my eye. I felt terribly foolish and wished they would hurry up and get it over with, which they did.

The gang gathered around my imaginary grave and tried to act sad. Little Jim, who had been picking wild flowers, brought a bouquet and laid them on my chest. I was really trying hard to keep a straight face when the flowers made me sneeze, and that made Little Jim giggle. Big Jim shushed us all and said in a very dignified tone, "Friends, let us pause in silence as we pay our respects to the memory of an old man who lived always a clean and respectable life . . ."

While everybody was quiet, I looked up through the branches of the different trees and saw a very pretty red squirrel. It was going from one branch to another, running along the top side of one, leaping across to another tree, and then following a long overhanging branch that extended out over the moss-covered roof of the house.

All of a sudden, I splintered the silence all to pieces by saying excitedly, "Hey, gang, look! There's a squirrel!"

That broke up our funeral, which had been long enough anyway. Besides, somehow it didn't seem right to play funeral, and we all felt better when it was over and I was alive again.

"I'll be a *ghost* now," I said, "and haunt Dragonfly." I let out a long wail that sounded like a loon I'd heard when we'd been up North.

But Dragonfly didn't think it was funny and said so. Then all of a sudden he got a strange, scared look on his face and said, "Hey, you guys, listen! I h–hear something. It—it's inside the house!"

Well, that was one of the reasons we had come up there in the first place—to convince Dragonfly there wasn't any such thing as a ghost. But he was a hard person to convince of anything. I looked at his worried forehead and noticed that he really almost believed there *was* a ghost. Just that second also, I saw him give his neck a quick twist, as if he was shaking his head "No." In fact it seemed he had been doing that every few minutes.

Even though you don't believe in any such thing as ghosts, when you have somebody in your gang who *does* believe in them and who actually is worried, it's sort of like a boy having the measles and the rest of his friends catching them from him. As much as I didn't believe in ghosts myself, a little later when we all were crowded up close to the door of that house and listening, and I heard a noise that sounded like something moving around in one of the rooms, I felt a creepy feeling go up and down my spine.

I noticed Little Jim was crowded up close to Big Jim and that he had the stick that he nearly always carried with him gripped terribly tight in his small hands.

Big Jim's face, with its seven or eight fuzzy hairs on its upper lip, looked pretty serious as he pressed his left ear close to the old white doorknob. He listened to what we could all hear even without being any closer—a sound of something moving around over a wooden floor.

I guess we never had been so quiet in our lives as we were right those few seconds while we listened. And then it seemed I was not only hearing the mysterious sound in the house, but there was a groaning noise up in the trees above us also. The wind was blowing a little, and the leaves of the trees were rustling, and I remembered what Dad had said at the supper table not long ago: "To him who is in fear, everything rustles," which was what some famous Greek poet had said over a thousand years ago.

Circus, who was very mischievous and didn't believe in ghosts any more than I did, all of a sudden called out in an excited voice, "Gang, I *see* it! I see it! Come here, quick!"

It's pretty shocking to your mind to have an excited voice call out like that right when you're all tense inside anyway, so I jumped as if I was shot, and so did most of us. We all looked behind us to where Circus was, maybe about fifteen feet away, not far from the old windmill tower. He was looking up and pointing.

I looked in the direction he was looking, expecting to see something. I didn't know what.

"Look and listen at the same time," he said. "See it? It's got two wooden limbs!"

"Two what?" Poetry squawked.

And in my mind's eye I was imagining a ridiculous-looking thing or person or animal, something with two wooden legs. And then I saw it, and it made me mad that Circus had got us all excited over nothing, but there it was as plain as anything, away up high, maybe sixty feet above us. Two big limbs of two great elm trees were sort of interlocked, and as the trees swayed in the wind, they made a sound that was almost like a ghost's groan.

Imagine that! It was one of the most let-down feelings I'd ever had and maybe was for all of us.

We all crowded up close to the house door again and listened and at the same time looked up toward the huge limbs of the elms as they swayed very slowly in the wind and rubbed against each other. Sure enough, the sounds were coming from up in the trees *above* the house and not from the inside as we'd thought.

Well, we'd solved the mystery of the haunted house, and right away we began to feel proud of ourselves and to talk about how silly people were to believe in ghosts. We knew we would have fun telling people about how we'd solved the mystery. It was time to go home anyway, so we all started.

"It couldn't have been Old Tom the Trap-per's ghost anyway," Little Jim said to us as we ran and walked and played leapfrog and hur-ried back up the creek toward our homes, "because my daddy told me the Bible says that, when a Christian dies, his spirit goes straight to heaven to be with Jesus. So what would he be doing hanging around an old house?"

But Dragonfly wasn't convinced. He said

with a pouting voice, "He might want to visit his buried body under the maple tree."

"Not Old Tom, I'll bet," Poetry said as he puffed along in his own chubby body beside me. "Anybody as good a Christian as he was—if he came back, he'd do something more important than groan and scare people. He'd want to try to make everybody a Christian," which made pretty good sense.

Well, that settled the haunted house idea for us until late that fall, when the hunting season on coon opened in the middle of November, and when it wasn't against the law to hunt coon with dogs. And that's the story I'll get going on real quick and tell you about as fast as I can. Boy oh boy! Those dogs really led us into the middle of an exciting adventure!

6

Before I go any farther, I'd better tell you about Dragonfly's tick. I knew by the way he couldn't help twisting his neck every now and then that maybe he ought to have somebody take him to a doctor. I found out more about it when Dad and Mom were talking one day. I happened to hear Mom say to Dad, "It gives me the blues every time I think of Dragonfly's tick. That's the worst one I ever saw a boy have."

I was out in our toolhouse at the time, trying to make a rustic cedar lamp. I had a wire brush, my Boy Scout knife, a wood auger, and some electric wire sockets. I was scraping off a twisted-up cedar knot, all the small knobs and pieces of wood and bark I didn't need, and digging into the crevices and cracks to get out the old dead parts.

I was making an electric lamp to give to my cousin Wally for Christmas. Wally was red-haired and freckled like me and lived in the city and was as dumb about the country as country boys are supposed to be about a city.

I had the wire brush in my hand and was brushing *with* the grain of the wood to get off all the dirt and dust, and Mom and Dad were just outside the door, not far from the grape arbor. Dad had pumped a pail of water for her. I'd stopped brushing just as he stopped pumping. They didn't hear me, or maybe they wouldn't have talked as they did.

When Mom said to Dad what I just said she said, which you can read again if you want to, Dad said, "Yes, that's one of the worst kind of ticks a boy ever gets."

In my mind's eye, I was seeing Circus's bluetick hound, and the thing didn't make sense at all until Mom said to Dad again, "Do you really think it's his parents' fault?"

And Dad said, "It could be. I talked with the doctor, and he says that when a boy has a tick —such as neck-twisting or shoulder-shrugging or throat-clearing or something like that —it nearly always means that his father or mother or maybe some other relative is picking at him too much. Always correcting him whenever he is anywhere around and making him feel that everything he does has something wrong with it. When the boy is what is called a 'good' boy and doesn't fight or talk back, the feelings inside him have to get out some way, so the boy's nerves backfire with a tick!"

Well, when my folks said that about Dragonfly, I thought about myself, and I was glad Mom and Dad knew what they knew. Right that second I understood a little better why Dad didn't punish me as often as he used to, and why they weren't always telling me every time I made a little mistake but were letting me just grow.

I didn't find out till later that you spelled the kind of tick Dragonfly had "t–i–c" instead of "t–i–c–k."

Well, just that minute I decided I would brush on my twisted cedar knot some more, which I did, thinking about what Mom and Dad had been saying and feeling sorry for Dragonfly. He really was a great guy, I thought, and he had nice parents too, and it was too bad they didn't know about tics and how to keep a boy from getting one.

Dad carried the pail of water into the house for Mom and then, hearing me brushing away on my knot, he came to the screen door and looked in and said, "Hi, Bill. How're you comin'?" Then he came in and watched me and, being a natural-born boy's father, he said, "Be sure to brush *with* the grain, or you'll have a rough surface."

Feeling mischievous, I all of a sudden said, "Better not correct me too much, Dad, or I'll get a tic, too, like Dragonfly."

Then I ducked my head, focused my eyes on my work, and brushed away harder than ever.

"You're a bright boy," Dad said.

And I said in the same mischievous voice he had used on me, "I know it. I'm Theodore Collins's son."

Just then Mom called from the back door for Dad to come and answer the telephone, which he did. I kept brushing away, feeling fine inside and liking my parents better than ever.

And now for the rest of the story about the haunted house.

It was, as I said, the middle of November before the season for hunting coon with dogs was open and we could hunt without its being against the law.

It had been a wonderful autumn, and we had been terribly busy at our house and also at our barn. When the first frost came in September, we'd harvested all our pumpkins, putting a lot of them in the cellar and also up in our attic for pumpkin pies in the winter and chopping up a lot of them for our cows. Dad and I worked harder than anything, getting ready for winter. We cut some of the corn and shocked it, and we drilled wheat in between the corn rows so it'd be in the ground early next spring, and we spread lime and fertilizer on our south pasture, getting a lot of the fertilizer from a pile behind our barn.

Mom and Poetry's mom worked together a lot, first at our house and then at theirs, getting all the cabbage heads out of the gardens and chopping them up very fine and packing them away in big jars in our different cellars. In the winter the cabbage would turn into sauerkraut, which I didn't like but which Mom said would be good for me to learn to like because it was good for me.

All the young roosters we'd raised that year learned to crow, and old Andrew Jackson got terribly jealous of them, and the young pullets started in laying middle-sized eggs. We also made apple cider and did a million other things a farmer has to do if he wants to save the things that have grown in his fields in the summer.

On Saturdays the gang got together when our parents would let us have a little time from all the work we had to do, and we gathered hickory nuts and walnuts. On Halloween we worked a few friendly tricks on our different parents but had sense enough not to hurt anybody's property. No matter how mischievous a boy is, if his parents or his teacher or somebody has taught him the Bible, he knows that it's just as bad a sin to *damage* anybody's property as it is to steal it—and stealing is a sin, and any boy is dumb to do it.

Finally, there came the night of the coon hunt and the wild, fierce, fast chase down the creek, past the old bare sycamore tree and farther on, past Old Man Paddler's cabin and on and on. We'd been following the dogs when, all of a sudden, we realized that we'd been going in the direction of the haunted house.

Of course, as you know, the gang had decided it *wasn't* haunted but that the groaning noise had been caused by the rubbing together of the limbs of two big elm trees away up above the old stone house's roof.

But the way Blue Jay acted when he struck that trail, and the way Circus's dad's other hound, big long-eared Blackie, galloped along with and all around old Blue Jay—both of them baying and bawling and acting wilder than they ever acted on a coon trail before—it was enough to scare almost any boy.

"Listen!" Circus said to all of us, and we stopped and listened. It was a very dark, cloudy night, and we couldn't see at all beyond the circle of our kerosene lantern lights.

It felt good to be hunting without any grown-ups with us. Circus's dad was sick, and the family needed money, and it would be a shame not to go coon hunting the first night of the open season. So Circus had helped Poetry and Dragonfly and Big Jim and me persuade our parents that it would be all right for us to take a little walk just to see if we could catch anything along Sugar Creek.

Big Jim, the oldest one of us, carried his .22 rifle, since most country boys who are old enough are allowed to use rifles to shoot squirrels and rabbits and rats.

Little Jim's parents let him go along too.

Most of us knew there wasn't any such thing as a ghost, but Dragonfly still thought there was. Just before we'd started that night, he said, "I hope we don't run into any ghosts."

I said, "Don't be a dumb bunny. There isn't any such thing."

"My mother *heard* a ghost last night and also one last week."

"What did he sound like?" Circus wanted to know.

And Dragonfly answered, "Mother said he just screamed a great big long scream like he was terribly mad or maybe scared."

Well, we knew Dragonfly's mother could hear a ghost without there being any, because she had that kind of an imagination. So when Dragonfly said that, Poetry, who is always doing something mischievous anyway, said to Dragonfly in an excited voice, "Hey, open your mouth quick! Let me look in!"

Poetry flashed his flashlight on Dragonfly and with his other hand made some quick up-and-down movements over his head and face.

At the same time, Dragonfly ducked his head and tried to dodge the light and said, "Hey! What're you doing?"

Poetry said, "Oh, nothing, I was just shaking salt on your words! Don't people always say that, when you can't believe what anybody says, you're supposed to take it with a grain of salt?"

We didn't have time to laugh or be mischievous right then, though, because now we had all stopped at the spring to look for coon tracks. We wanted to see if maybe some big papa or mama coon or some of their children had been there washing a late supper. But there weren't any tracks at all.

All of a sudden I heard a long, wild bawl away up the creek in the direction of the North Road bridge, and Dragonfly let out a cry and said, "There, that's it. That's what my mother heard!"

"It's Blackie!" Circus cried excitedly. "He's hit a coon trail. Come on, gang!" He swung around, stepped across the cement basin, leaped across the mud puddle on the other side, and dashed up the hill. He passed the hanging linden tree with all of us following him. It was natural for Circus instead of Big Jim to take the lead in a coon chase.

Just that minute it seemed that old Blue Jay also had smelled trail, because he opened up with his different-pitched bawl. It was very long and had a little tail on it at the end, and it sounded like *"Ooooo—woo! Ooooo—woo!"*

Then both dogs cut loose in one bawl after another, sounding like a dog duet turning handsprings and somersaults.

Up the hill we all went, swinging our lanterns and flashlights and hurrying as fast as we could.

It was Poetry who thought of it first. He and I were puffing and panting along behind and in front of and beside each other. He said to me, "Listen, Bill, it sounded like they struck the trail at the very place where Old Tom the Trapper was shot!"

I got a funny feeling up and down my spine when I heard that and said, "It sounds like two ghosts—a blue-ticked one and a black-and-tan one."

Circus and Big Jim, running ahead of us, kept yelling back to us littler guys, "Hurry up, you! They're trailing fast!"

And we kept on hurrying.

After what seemed a terribly long chase, Circus stopped stock-still in his tracks up ahead and said, "Listen, everybody. Old Jay's chopping. Hear him? He's chopping at a tree!"

"Chopping!" Dragonfly exclaimed. "A dog chopping at a tree?"

We all stopped and listened, and the dog's voice we heard was as different as night and day from Blue Jay's long squalling bawl of a while ago. It was coming in short, quick, excited barks now. A minute later we heard a higher-pitched voice doing the same thing. I knew that was Blackie and that their new and different kind of bark was their way of telling us that whatever it was they had been trailing had run up a tree and for us to hurry up and come, which is the way coonhounds do.

Little Jim answered Dragonfly's question by saying in a mischievous voice, "Sure. They're trying to chop the tree down for us."

Of course, they weren't. Circus explained it to Dragonfly, saying, "That's a word the man used when he sold old Blue Jay to my pop. He said that Jay *bawled* when he opened up on the trail and that he *chopped* when he had chased the coon up a tree."

Well, we dashed on, leaping over logs and swerving around brush piles, on and on and on. Long ago we had crossed the branch and passed the sycamore tree and the cave. Then we were up into the hills past Old Man Paddler's cabin. Still the dogs chased on, farther and farther, with us right after them, not realizing at first how far from home we were.

And then all of a sudden Poetry startled me by exclaiming in a short-breathed, excited voice, "Hey! I'll bet you they're barking at the old maple tree by Old Tom the Trapper's grave!"

Everybody must've heard Poetry say that, especially Dragonfly, who said, "I *told* you it was a ghost!"

7

It took only a few more minutes of running and scrambling around trees and bushes and brier patches and clambering up and down little hills for us to get to where old Blue Jay and Blackie were acting like two wild things. They were leaping and chopping in their different-pitched voices around the base of the old maple tree. They were looking up and barking and jumping and stopping to look at us and panting with their long tongues hanging out of their mouths and acting important because they had treed a coon or whatever it was.

I quick shot the long beam of my dad's flashlight up into the tree and swished the light all around, looking for a patch of brownish fur, which is what you expect to see if a coon is up a tree. Or maybe you'd see a pale yellowish tail with six or seven black rings around it. If he isn't too high up, and you get a good look at him, you can maybe see his white whiskers, which are like a cat's whiskers, and also the rest of his face. Most coons have black cheeks and a dark stripe that runs all the way up and down their foreheads.

As soon as anybody saw him, we'd tell Big Jim, and he, being a good shot, would shoot him right out of the tree for us. Mr. Coon would come crashing down through the bare branches to the ground. If he was still alive and a fierce fighter, old Blue Jay and Blackie would still be able to lick him. If Big Jim's bullet killed him, we'd make the dogs leave him alone so that the fur wouldn't be damaged, and the night's hunt would be over.

Right beside me Big Jim was loading his new rifle. For a second I watched him, noticing that it was a very nice rifle with a walnut stock and a long dark-blue barrel with an open rear sight and a blade front sight. I'd seen him load a gun many a time when some of us had gone rabbit or squirrel hunting with him, and he always kept it pointed away from everybody and at the ground while he was doing it.

The dogs were making so much noise and acting so excited that we couldn't hear much of anything. When Circus tried to stop them they would quit for a few seconds, but before we could listen long enough to hear any suspicious sounds—if there had been any to hear—one or the other of the hounds would start chopping at the tree again.

"Here," Circus said to Big Jim, "let me have the gun. I'll stop 'em from barking." He walked over to Big Jim, reached out his hand for the rifle, and I thought, *What on earth!* Circus acted as if he was mad, too.

Big Jim had just finished loading the .22. I was surprised to see him hand it over to Circus, just as Little Jim called out in an anxious voice, "What you going to do—shoot the *dogs?*"

"Wait and see—and listen," Circus said. The next thing I knew he had the gun to his shoulder. He was pointing it up toward the branches of the tree and sighting as though he was going to shoot something. I thought different things, such as maybe he had already seen the coon and was going to shoot it.

"Now, listen, everybody!" Circus ordered, and we did.

Both dogs stopped chopping, and both of them had their eyes on Circus and the gun, waiting for him to shoot. He didn't but just kept on pointing while all of us listened—which is the way to get a coon dog to stop barking.

I didn't know what I expected to hear, if anything—maybe the rubbing together of the branches of the big elm trees overhead, the groaning sounds that we'd heard one day during the summer, or else maybe the scratching of a coon's claws on the bark of the tree, if there *was* a coon and if it might be still climbing higher.

Of course, Dragonfly was probably listening for a ghost, although when he'd found out that the sound his mother had heard was either old Blue Jay or Blackie bawling along Sugar Creek, he hadn't been so *sure* that there was a ghost.

If anybody had been actually *in* the old stone house looking out through one of the dirty windows, he could have seen a very interesting gang of different-sized, different-looking boys.

If he'd looked at Little Jim, he'd have seen one of the cutest kids that ever wore a brand-new, brown plaid zipper jacket. Little Jim had both his hands shoved into the jacket's side pockets, and I could tell by the two bulges they made that his fists were doubled up, which meant he was maybe kind of nervous and also a little bit afraid, although if his fists were doubled up he might feel braver than if they weren't.

Dragonfly just that second was holding a red handkerchief up to his nose, maybe trying to stop a sneeze. It was the kind of handkerchief that is very large, almost two feet square, like the bandanas farmers and hunters sometimes use. Even some of the women and girls around Sugar Creek used them—only not to stop sneezes but to wear on their heads, the way they do scarves.

Poetry had on a heavy, red sheep-lined corduroy coat that had its zipper unfastened and was hanging open because he was pretty hot after our chase. His red corduroy cap had its ear flaps turned up, and one of his ears was flopped over.

I was thinking those things about how different ones of us looked or would look to anybody inside that old house—or even to a ghost if there was one. Also, there was a quick flash of thought in my mind that wondered why everybody always thought a ghost had to wear something white and long like a bedsheet, instead of ordinary clothes.

All of a sudden, while everything was as quiet as death, I heard a banging noise, a little like a gun going off, and also like a door slamming somewhere. I knew it wasn't Circus's gun. The sound came from the house itself.

We all jumped as if we had been shot at, and I quickly flashed the light of my flashlight in the direction of the old house. We had all heard it, and I guess we all also saw what we saw at the same time. Anyway Dragonfly and I did, because we both said in scared whispering voices, "*Sh!* There's a light in the old house!"

Imagine that! First a banging noise like a door slamming, and then suddenly it happens—on a very dark night when you're thinking about a ghost anyway and are out in a lonely forest just outside a house that some people believe is haunted. There in front of your eyes as you look through a dirty window-pane not more than thirty feet from you, you see a light of some kind!

What to do, or what *not* to do, was the question.

Dragonfly was the first to speak—half yell, rather—exclaiming, "It's a real ghost! Let's get out of here!"

Well, as anybody knows, when one boy catches the measles, and there are a lot of other boys around when he does, the other boys are bound to get the measles too. So when Dragonfly let out a scared yell, saying, "It's a real ghost! Let's get out of here!" his being scared was as contagious as measles. I'll have to admit that I wanted to get out of there as fast as I could myself.

You know a boy would rather be brave than most anything else—anyway, he can't stand to have anyone think he is a coward, and sometimes he'll say he *isn't* scared even when he is. He doesn't even stop to think it isn't the truth when he says, "*Me* scared? Don't be silly!"

Sometimes on a rainy day when I'm out in our barn sitting by an open window and the rain is pouring down on our shingled roof and I am cracking and eating black walnuts, I like to imagine I am *two* boys instead of *one*. I talk and argue with myself about different things. Old Man Paddler, who tells all kinds of interesting stories about the Sugar Creek of long ago, sometimes tells us that a Christian boy has what the Bible calls two natures. One of them is *bad*, and the other is *good*. The good one is called the *new* nature, which only saved people have, and it's up to us whether we live a good life or a bad one.

Well, when we heard that noise inside the house, part of me was scared, and the other part of me said it was silly to be scared, that there wasn't any such thing as a ghost. But when Dragonfly started to run back toward the creek, yelling for us to follow him, before I knew I was going to do it, I had turned and was shooting after him as fast as the arrow making a beeline for Old Tom the Trapper's chest.

But we got stopped with Big Jim's gruff half-brave and half-scared voice barking at us savagely, saying, "Stop! Let's don't be a bunch of silly superstitious cowards! Let's go inside and see what's going on in there!"

8

When Big Jim says something like that to us, there isn't a member of the Sugar Creek Gang that's too afraid to stick with him.

Of course, a light inside the house could mean only one thing, I thought. There had to be somebody in there that could turn on a flashlight, because that's exactly what the light had looked like when I'd seen it.

We had a hard time making the hounds keep still. They were absolutely sure that the "whatever it was" was up the tree. But if it *had* been, it certainly wasn't up there anymore, I thought. We'd shined our lights all around up in the tree and hadn't spotted a thing that looked like an animal. Since it was the fall of the year with all the branches bare of leaves, if any wild animal *had* been up there we'd have seen it.

"You m—mean w—we are g—going inside?" Dragonfly stammered, right after Big Jim had said we were.

Big Jim, who wasn't afraid of much of anything said, "We are! Everybody follow me." With that he picked up his lantern and started around the side of the house to where we knew there was a door.

"How'll we get in?" Poetry asked in his

squawky, ducklike voice—which for some reason seemed extra squawky.

And Big Jim answered, "I've got a key."

"A key!" I said and so said several of us at the same time. "Where'd you get a key?"

"Old Man Paddler gave it to me," he said. "He bought this old house last month, and he has hired my dad and me to come in and clean it up. He's going to make a Sugar Creek Gang Bible camp out of it, and every year in the summer there'll be a special camp for boys, who can come from all over the country and stay here for almost nothing."

That certainly sounded great to me. It would be a grand thing if every boy in the world could go to a Bible camp once or twice while he was still a boy.

But right that minute, when there was a ghost in the old house waiting to jump out at us any minute, there wasn't any time to think about a boys' camp, especially since Big Jim had the key out of his pocket and was walking right up to that door to unlock it.

For a change, the hounds were quiet. In fact, they were right behind and between different ones of us. I noticed old Jay had the hair on his back standing straight up, which is the way a dog's hair acts when there is a strange human being around or else a stray dog or cat or something else.

First, Big Jim knocked on the old door, which is good etiquette. It is polite and also good sense for a boy to always knock on a door and wait for an answer before going in.

I held my breath, remembering the banging noise that we'd heard a few minutes before and also the light I'd seen inside when I looked through the very dirty glass window.

Knock-knock-knock-knock—four firm, half-fierce knocks, like a policeman's knocking on a gangster's door. I knew that Big Jim was maybe imagining himself to be a policeman or a detective or a sheriff, which boys always like to pretend to be anyway.

Even the hounds kept quiet as we all listened.

"Open up!" Big Jim said and knocked again.

And then, as clear as broad daylight, I heard a sound from inside the house—a banging noise like the one we'd heard before.

Beside me, Blue Jay got a low fierce growl in his throat. And Blackie, standing beside Circus, who held him by his collar, had a growl in his throat also, and his coal-black hair was straight up on his back.

Boy oh boy, what was going to happen next? I wondered.

And then Big Jim called in a gruff voice, "We're coming in!" He shoved the key into the lock and turned it—or rather tried to, but it wouldn't turn.

"The lock's rusted, I'll bet you," he said as he tried it again and again.

Well sir, try as we would, we couldn't get that door unlocked.

"We've got to get inside," Big Jim said. "We've

got to prove to ourselves that there isn't any such thing as a ghost. Besides, I don't think anybody heard a banging noise anyway. When a guy's afraid of a ghost, everything he hears sounds like one!"

And I remembered again what Dad had quoted from some Greek guy who'd lived a long time ago: "To him who is in fear, everything rustles."

"But I saw a *light*," I said. "I *know* I did."

"Anybody *else* see a light?" Big Jim asked over his shoulder, and Dragonfly stuck up for me by saying, "*I* did. It went on and off like a flashlight."

Since the key wouldn't unlock the door, we went around and tried different windows to see if they'd open, and they wouldn't.

Then Circus spied a broken stairway that looked as if it led down to a cellar. He made a dive down the steps and gave a shove to the very old door at the bottom. The door gave a little. He shoved again, and it burst open.

We all decided to go down into the cellar to see if there was any ghost down there. And that's how we happened to get up into the house itself. While we were down in the creepy old cellar, which was musty and had spiderwebs stretched across its corners and hanging from its ceiling, we found another stairway going up. When we pushed on the door in the ceiling at the top of the stairs, we found that it was loose. We shoved it up a little, and, sure enough, it was what we thought it was—a trapdoor that led right up into one of the rooms of the old haunted house.

In less than almost no time, with our hearts pounding with excitement, we had clambered up that rickety stairway and were inside.

It certainly wasn't anything much to look at—just a room that had maybe been a kitchen, another that had probably been a living room, and another a bedroom or a dining room or something, and two other big wide rooms, each one having loose plaster and cobwebs and dirt on the floor and some old-fashioned chairs.

We shined our lights all around to see what we could see, while Jay with his blue ticks all over him and Blackie scurried from room to room ahead of us, smelling everything and every corner to see if they could smell anything suspicious, which both of them seemed to, because they still acted excited and worried and kept sniffing at the walls and whimpering.

I studied Big Jim's face to see if he was worried, and he wasn't. In fact, his face had a kind of a smirk. "Well," he said in a bored voice, "we know what caused the light Bill thought he saw, and now if we can find out what made the noise Dragonfly thought he heard, we will have proved there isn't any ghost."

It made me mad to hear him calmly say that. I knew I'd seen a light flash on and off, and it didn't feel very good to have my idea squelched and be made to look like a dope, so I said, "You don't know anything of the kind."

"Oh, I don't, don't I?" Big Jim said. He

flashed his light over toward a wall and onto an old rectangular mirror hanging there.

"See that!" he said. He flashed his light on and off a few times, and I saw the reflection of his light in the mirror. I noticed also that the mirror was in line with the window, and I knew that when I was outside and had flashed my light into the window that it had shone onto this old mirror. It had been the light of my own flashlight I'd seen. I was disgusted, because I wanted there to be somebody inside this old house.

Of course, it didn't matter so much that Dragonfly had thought he heard a banging noise. We all expected *him* to hear things.

"You'll have to prove to Jay and Blackie that they don't smell anything then," I said. "Look at 'em. They're acting awfully funny."

And they were. Right that second, Blue Jay, who'd been sniffing and whimpering in a very worried dog voice, came to a stairway that led to the upstairs of the old house. Quick as a flash he started sniffing his way up, with Blackie right after him.

9

Imagine that! Old Blue Jay was on his way up a mysterious stairway with Blackie right after him, both of them sniffing at the steps as though they were following some kind of wild animal's trail. They were going up fast, and I knew that in a jiffy we'd all be following them!

No sooner had Jay and Blackie disappeared up that spooky stairs and we heard their feet galloping around from room to room, than we were on our way up too.

It certainly wasn't much to look at up there. The first room was just a small bare room big enough for a boy's bed and a dresser. We hurried through that empty little room, on past an open wardrobe door, and came out into a large room that was as empty as the other one and the downstairs had been.

Blue Jay and Blackie were acting as though whatever they had thought was up here wasn't here now. They were running from one corner to another, whimpering and not paying any attention to us and worrying in their dog voices. They reminded me of my brown-and-gray-haired mother when she loses a fountain pen or maybe one of her four overstuffed handbags somewhere in the house and can't find it and is afraid she's left it somewhere, and all of us, including Dad and me, have to stop what we're doing or reading or talking or thinking about and help Mom until she finds it right where she thought it was in the first place.

We looked in the wardrobe, flashing our lights all around, and I noticed that there was a row of wooden pegs sticking out of one wall about as high as Big Jim's head, which I decided were used to hang people's clothes on.

"Nothing but a row of wooden clothes hangers," I said and reached up and caught hold of one, remembering there were pegs like them in our barn at home that the men who had built our barn had used to pin some big logs together.

I used to catch hold of the ones in our barn and hoist myself up on top of a high log and then use the log for an imaginary springboard from which I turned flip-flops on the hay. That is, I *used* to until one day Dad caught me at it and made me stop, saying gruffly, "William Collins, that hay is the horses' and cows' meat and potatoes and Jello pudding! How would you like some wild animal to roll and tumble around all over *your* supper just before you ate it?" For some reason I hadn't wanted to hear that because it spoiled my playing in the hay, and for a few minutes I wasn't only cross at Dad but at both our horses and cows for being so particular about their food.

Before I got through thinking those terribly fast thoughts, Little Jim interrupted me by saying, "Look! There's a peg real low down for a *boy* to hang his coat on."

Sure enough there was. It was about three feet from the wardrobe's floor, away over in a corner all by itself. Little Jim was always noticing something like that, I thought, things that none of the rest of us saw.

"I'll bet the little boy liked to live in this nice big house," Little Jim said, and when I looked at him he had a faraway expression in his eyes as though he wasn't even with us but his thoughts were back in the days of long ago. Maybe he was even imagining himself to be that little boy and hanging his brand-new brown plaid zipper jacket on that little round peg in the corner of the wardrobe.

Right away we started looking all around the large room, which didn't even have a mirror hanging on its wall. We searched through the drawers of a very old-looking writing desk, which was the only furniture the upstairs had. There wasn't a thing in them, although one drawer looked as if a mouse or maybe twenty-five or thirty mice had been using it for a place to play roughhouse. Some old newspapers on the bottoms of the drawers had been chewed to small pieces.

Just as Big Jim slammed the last drawer shut, it made a banging noise, and Dragonfly cried out excitedly, "There! That's what I heard —that banging noise. There *was* somebody up here awhile ago."

Well, it was a ridiculous idea, and we said so.

Big Jim opened and shut the drawer a half dozen times to show Dragonfly his idea was crazy. Then, looking at his watch, he said all of a sudden, "Say, our folks will be worried about us. We'd better beat it for home!" With that, he started back toward the other room and the stairs.

But Dragonfly must have felt he was being belittled, and he wasn't satisfied. He said, "You guys don't give a ghost a ghost of a chance to prove that he is a ghost. Don't you know ghosts have to have it pitch-dark before you can see them?"

Well, it was an idea, and we took Dragonfly up on it. Big Jim lifted his kerosene lantern to the level of his eyes, turned the wick down, pressed on the lever that lifted the globe, gave a quick puff of breath, and out went his lantern. Circus did the same thing to his. "OK, gang, off with all your flashlights, and everybody be quiet and listen and look for all you're worth and see if anybody sees a ghost."

"Or *hears* one," Poetry said, emphasizing the word "hears" in his squawky ducklike voice.

"You sound like one yourself," I said.

We took Jay and Blackie by their collars to keep them from running around and making a noise. Circus held his dad's black-and-tan dog, and I held Blue Jay. I squatted low, holding onto Jay's new leather collar with my bare hands.

Talk about it being dark enough to see a ghost! That was the blackest dark I ever saw in my whole life. Not a one of us moved, not even the dogs, although I could feel Blue Jay trembling and knew he was wondering what on earth was going on and why. I could hear different ones of us breathing, but that was all.

I was listening for some sound outside the house, such as the rubbing together of the two elm limbs away up above the roof, but there wasn't any sound of rubbing because there wasn't any wind blowing.

I could smell the smoky smell that you always smell after a kerosene lantern has been blown out—the wick always smokes a little. Since my face was close to old Blue Jay's new leather collar, I could smell that and also Jay himself. For a second I wondered how a dog could smell an animal's track well enough to follow it at night when he couldn't see it.

Just then somebody whispered, "Hurry up, ghost, and show yourself. We've got to get going home."

Still not a sound, except the breathing of six boys and two dogs, and only the smell of wick smoke and a leather dog collar and the two dogs and also the kind of old musty smell of the house itself.

And then, all of a sudden, I heard something behind me, behind the wall I was crouched down beside! Blue Jay must have heard it at the same time, because I felt him suddenly get nervous and the hair on his back start to bristle, and I knew there was actually something somewhere making some kind of a noise, and it wasn't being made by any member of the Sugar Creek Gang.

"*Sh!*" Big Jim said, shushing us.

But we were already shushed.

Circus whispered in a rough whisper, "Jay! Keep quiet."

I knew it wasn't old Blue Jay. It was something behind both of us, and it wasn't in the room but was on the other side of the wall.

It just didn't seem possible that I was hearing what I was hearing, and yet I was . . . no, I wasn't either, because right that minute the noise stopped, and there was only our own breathing and the deathly silence of that old musty-smelling stone house.

Big Jim's husky whisper broke the silence with the question, "You guys hear anything?"

Several of us said in the same kind of husky whisper, "Yeah! Something right behind the wall somewhere."

Little Jim spoke up then, and his voice in the darkness sounded awfully cute as he said, "I heard something *scratching* on something."

And the second he said it, I knew that was what I had heard also, and I said so. I kept listening and straining my eyes in several different directions to see if I could see anything that looked like a ghost is supposed to look, but I couldn't.

Poetry spoke up from beside or behind me somewhere and said, "It sounded like a rat gnawing on an ear of corn."

His idea sounded cuckoo. In my mind's eye

I wasn't seeing anything as small as a mere rat but some great big fierce wild animal of some kind. If it was only a rat, I'd have to change my mind, and I didn't want to do it. That is one of the hardest things in the world to do anyway, Dad says—to get a person whose mind is already made up to change it.

We listened a while longer and didn't hear anything, so we turned on our flashlights, lit our lanterns, and disappointedly made our way to the stairs, not having seen any ghost and only having heard something like a rat scratching.

Poetry and I were the last ones to go down the stairs. He stopped me with a tug on my arm and a whisper in my ear. We waited until the gang and the hounds had made their noisy boy-and-dog way downstairs and were walking around down there. Then he whispered and said, "Let's see if we can see anything. If it's a ghost, it's maybe afraid of so *many* people. It's probably used to living here all alone, and a lot of noisy boys and dogs scare it—*sh!* Listen! "

I really listened. Both of us had our lights out, and I was looking all around, but there wasn't a sight or a sound.

Poetry sighed and started quoting the poem called "The Night Before Christmas," which somebody had written long ago. This is the way it begins:

> 'Twas the night before Christmas,
> And all through the house,

Not a creature was stirring,
Not even a mouse . . .

It certainly was disappointing, but as Big Jim had said a while ago, it was time for us all to get going home or our folks would worry about us, as grown-ups do about their boys or girls and can't help it, the way our old cow always worries about her calf when it's away from her and she wants to get to where it is and can't.

Just as Poetry got to the place where he said, "Not a creature was stirring, not even a *mouse*" —just as he said "mouse"—I heard something honest-to-goodness for sure, and I stopped Poetry's poetry with a quick, snappy shush, adding, "Listen again!"

The sound was a panting and a growling noise at the same time, and I knew that somewhere close to us was a wild animal of some kind.

Our flashlights were still out, and I tell you my dad's long flash went on again in as quick a hurry as Poetry's did. We also grabbed hold of each other to be sure we were both there and all right, and we were.

That settled *that*. There might not be any ghost, but there was *something* honest-to-goodness for sure in that old stone house, and it wasn't more than a half-dozen feet from where I was right that minute. And yet I couldn't see it.

"It sounded like it was in that old wardrobe," Poetry said. With his light on he wobbled his roly-poly self toward it.

We'd all looked in it a little while before, and it had been empty, but Poetry and I decided to look again. I swished my light all around the bare walls, and there still wasn't a thing in it except the row of wooden pegs and that one small lonesome little peg that had been just the right height for Little Jim to hang his clothes on.

"Whatever it is, it's behind the wall somewhere," Poetry said. "Maybe back in an attic, if there is one."

Sure, I thought. *There ought to be an attic. Nearly every house in the world has an attic of some kind.*

I looked with a frowning forehead at that empty wardrobe, at the row of empty wooden pegs, and also at the one small peg all by itself. And suddenly I remembered that Old Tom the Trapper hadn't had any children to hang clothes on a low peg. Before I knew what I was going to do, I had done it. I grabbed hold of the low-down wooden peg as if it was a handle to something and gave a sharp sideways pull on it. And the whole back wall of that wardrobe moved a little, making a dark crack opening into an attic!

Right away I knew that whole back wall of the wardrobe was a sliding panel and that back in there somewhere was the wild animal we'd heard growling and panting.

"Wait!" Poetry exclaimed behind me. "Don't slide it open any further, or it'll jump out and get away—or maybe eat us up!"

I quick shoved hard on the wooden peg, and the sliding door went shut with a bang, sounding exactly like the banging noise I'd heard before when we'd all been outside by the old maple tree.

Boy oh boy! Who or what was back in that dark attic? And what would happen next?

10

As soon as Poetry and I discovered there was an honest-to-goodness-for-sure attic in that old stone house and had slammed the sliding door shut, we must have made a lot of noise—such a clatter that the rest of the gang came scrambling back up to see what was the matter.

It wasn't easy to keep Blue Jay and Blackie under control, because a dog is like a boy when there is any excitement—he wants to get right into the middle of it. In fact, he wants to be a part of it himself.

Of course, we might need the dogs if there was a very big, fierce wild animal back in that dark attic, but we didn't want them to make a mad dash inside ahead of us until we could look in with our flashlights and see for ourselves what was there.

"You guys let me have a look in first," Big Jim ordered. He slid the panel open far enough to shove his flashlight in and take a peek, while the rest of us including the excited dogs stayed back and waited. He flashed his light all around first, then said, "Looks as bare as Old Mother Hubbard's cupboard. Might as well all go in and see if there are any bones for our poor dogs."

Dragonfly, who was behind Little Jim who

was behind me, heard Big Jim say "bare" and spoke up in a half-scared voice. "If it's a great big grizzly bear, what'll we do?"

Pretty soon, after different ones of us had looked in, we all decided that there wasn't anything to be afraid of. Making the dogs stay outside by shutting them in the smaller room, we all stooped down a little and went into the big spooky attic, in the center of which was a large square brick chimney.

If the attic had ever been used for a storeroom, whoever had lived here last had taken everything out except an old-fashioned spool bedstead, an old spinning wheel, some pairs of very old shoes, and some ears of yellow corn, which were scattered around on the floor. There was also a kind of dead smell as if something had died in there, but that was maybe because the attic had been closed up for so long that it had gotten to smell that way, I thought.

"Here are the bones for our poor dogs," Big Jim said, and when I looked where he had his light focused on the floor not far from the red brick chimney, I saw what looked like the bones and feathers of a dead chicken but nothing that looked like a live wild animal.

"S'pose maybe Old Tom the Trapper kept his chickens up here, and when he died the chickens starved to death?" Little Jim asked in his cute curious voice.

Big Jim was studying the bones and the feathers, and I could see the muscles of his jaw working. "This chicken was alive less than a week ago," he said seriously, and for the first time he seemed to have a note in his voice that sounded as if he thought there *was* something really mysterious about things. "See," he said, holding the bone of a drumstick in one hand and shining his flashlight right on it, "this chicken has been eaten *raw*. If it had been cooked, there wouldn't be signs of blood on it."

"Do g—ghosts eat *raw* chickens?" Dragonfly asked, which was almost as dumb a question as he'd ever asked.

Little Jim picked up an ear of corn and was studying it. I noticed he was looking at it as though it was as important as some kind of wildflower and he was going to write a note about it for our teacher.

"See!" he said. "This ear has exactly twenty-two rows of grains around it."

"What *of* it?" I said, and so did Dragonfly. We were all more interested in what Big Jim was doing and what he was going to decide. I could hear Blue Jay and Blackie in their room making whimpering noises as if they had been terribly mistreated by not being allowed to come in with us.

Little Jim answered Dragonfly and me by saying, "It's important. Just like it's important that all the mayapple flowers have exactly six petals and exactly twice as many stamens in their centers."

"It's *not* important," Dragonfly answered him crossly. "Not when there's a ghost or a wild animal been in here—maybe still *is* here."

Just then Big Jim, who had walked around to the other side of the chimney, let out a low whistle and said with a hiss, "Come over here, you guys, and have a look at this, will you!"

We scrambled over to him, and I noticed quick as a flash that there was a big hole in the side of the chimney where some bricks were missing. In fact, they were lying scattered around on the board floor. Then I saw what Big Jim had called us to look at—scratches and scratches and still more scratches on the softish red bricks and around the edge of the hole where they had been in the chimney. And also a lot of loose, brownish hair fastened to them.

It was plain as day that some animal had squeezed through that hole. Whatever had been in the attic had probably heard us coming and had gone up that chimney like a scared Santa Claus and had gotten away.

Thinking that, I spoke out loud and said, "Maybe old Santa Claus made a mistake and came down the wrong chimney, and when he tried to get out, he got stuck and burst the hole in the side and some of the fur on his suit came off."

Nobody seemed to think what I had said was funny, and nobody laughed.

Half disgusted, I flashed my light around at different things such as the bricks on the floor, the chicken bones and feathers, and the ears of corn. Some of the ears had teeth marks on them as if they'd been gnawed on.

Then I quickly shone my light into different dark corners of the attic and almost jumped out of my wits when I saw what I saw. Two very bright, shining *fiery* eyes were looking at me from away back in a corner where the attic floor and the roof met. In that same second I saw the broad face of some kind of wild animal. It had white whiskers, I noticed, and black cheeks and a black stripe all the way up and down the center of its forehead. Then it ducked down below the end of the floor and disappeared.

"It's a coon!" I yelled to the gang. "I saw it with my own eyes. A great big coon as big as a grizzly bear!"

Talk about excitement! I still had my flashlight focused on the place where the coon had dropped down into a hole below the ceiling slant at the end of the floor. Not knowing just how the old house had been built, I imagined she had a special hiding place down there on top of the rock siding.

Just that second, up came that big wide head again, and I saw those same two fiery eyes!

Dragonfly saw it, too, and hissed in a scared whisper, "It's a bear!"

Quick as a flash down went the white-whiskered coon's face, and there wasn't a thing left for us to see except the empty corner again.

"What'll we do?" different ones said to us. I

thought about what a terribly big coon it was and how much money it would sell for, so that Circus's family of nearly all girls could have groceries for another week.

"Let's shoot her," Big Jim said. "You guys shine your flashlights into that corner, and the very next time she looks up, I'll plug her"—which was a very good idea. That is, it *would* have been if it had worked.

But Mama Coon—or Papa, whichever it was—wouldn't accommodate us. No matter what we did or how much noise we made, she stayed down where she was.

It was Circus who thought of getting a long stick to see if by poking around a little we could stir her up and make her come out where Big Jim could shoot her. In a minute or so Circus was outdoors and back in again with a long, slender pole. With all the rest of us behind or away off to the side of Big Jim so we wouldn't be where the gun's bullet could hit us, Circus took his pole and poked away back where the coon had last been seen.

And then is when it happened. Boy oh boy! Mrs. Coon came out of her hiding place in the fastest second I ever saw, the way our old Mixy cat sometimes dashes wildly out of *her* hiding place when she's excited about something. Before any of us could have done anything to stop her, even if we could have moved that fast, she made a dive across the attic floor—a flash of beautiful brown fur, the biggest coon I'd ever seen and certainly big enough to have made all the large tracks we'd seen that summer at the spring. She hurled herself straight toward the chimney right beside which I was standing and made for the opening in the bricks, wiggled her fat, furry body through, and disappeared up the chimney.

A second later we heard a scrambling out on the roof, and I knew she was gone, maybe to a big tree somewhere where there would be another den to hide in.

Even before I had time to be sorry for Circus's family's sake that she had gotten away, I felt kind of glad, because any coon that was as smart as that deserved to get away.

Well, it was time to make a fast start for home, or our parents would worry too much about our being out so late, and it was not fair to a boy's parents for him to make them worry.

Just before we left that attic, we took a final look around at things, and Little Jim picked up a few ears of corn to take home. "For a souvenir," he explained when Dragonfly asked him what he wanted them for.

"I'll bet she's been coming in through that hole in the chimney bringing corn and chickens to her coon children, who maybe have a nest back there somewhere," Poetry's ducklike voice squawked.

"Yeah," Little Jim said, "just like Santa Claus coming down the chimney with toys."

"But how'd she get up on the roof in the first place?" Dragonfly wanted to know, as, a little later, all of us came out of the cellar door-way into the outdoors and started to go home.

"Easy as falling off a log," Circus said. "She climbs up that old maple tree, crawls out on that big overhanging limb away up yonder—right where my flashlight is shining this very second—and drops off. Like I said, just as easy as falling off a log. Then she zips up the outside of the chimney, and in she goes."

And that was that. We all believed it, and away we went toward home, making the dogs stay with us on the two leashes that Circus had brought with him. It would never do for Blue Jay and Blackie to strike the coon's trail again and have another wild chase through the woods to the maple tree. It'd be the same thing over again.

It was a very excited, very happy, and also very tired gang of boys that scrambled along in the light of our lanterns and flashlights back up the creek to our different homes.

Little Jim, who was walking beside Dragon-fly, was arguing with him about something. "Count 'em yourself," I heard him say to Dragonfly. "There's just exactly twenty-two on *this* one and exactly twenty on *this* one and exactly eighteen on *this* one."

I looked over at him, and he had in his hands the three ears of yellow corn that he'd picked up in that old attic.

I listened to Dragonfly ask him again, "What of it?"

And Little Jim said, "It proves that the One

who made the flowers and the ears of corn has a special plan—that He never makes twenty-one rows of corn around an ear, or seventeen, or nineteen, but always an *even* number instead of an *odd* one."

"I still don't see what of it," I heard Dragonfly say, but I noticed that his voice didn't sound as if he was as disgusted with Little Jim as he had been.

And as we all rambled along in the dancing shadows, I had one of the happiest feelings I ever had in my life. The One who made everything in nature was more wonderful than anything in the whole world. And I was glad that one day in the haymow of our barn I had given my heart to Him, which I told you all about a long time ago in my very first story, *The Swamp Robber.*

Boy oh boy! When I wrote that exciting story, I never had any idea how many other exciting adventures would happen to us or that I'd find time to tell you about them.

Even as I get ready to put a period at the end of this story, I'm remembering another interesting adventure that was different from any we'd ever had. If Big Jim hadn't been along with us on it, we all might have died, and that would have been the end of the Sugar Creek Gang. I was certainly glad that Big Jim had brought his .22 rifle along that day. If he hadn't, our lives wouldn't have been saved.

Maybe I'll have time to write that story for you next. I hope so.

The *Sugar Creek Gang* Series: